MY LOVER'S NECKTIE

Eve Healy

Content Warnings:

This is a work of fiction, but it does contain depictions and mentions of age gaps, power imbalances, social gaps, and BDSM.

CHAPTER ONE

Putting the key in the lock was more terrifying and yet satisfying than I had anticipated. Having the keys and getting access to what would be my life's goal was exciting, but the monthly rent of $2,000 was daunting. For the past year, I had been steadily growing my business, selling pieces I had sewn myself online, offering commissions, and occasionally doing tailoring jobs for friends or local businesses. I was bringing in a steady income at this point, enough to set aside for the licensing, permits, insurance, and the security deposit. It left me just enough to get a few yards of satin, silk, cashmere, cotton, and linens in various patterns.

So, with a sewing machine balanced on my hip, unruly yards of fabric tucked against my shoulder, and a box of pins clutched in my other hand, I turned the key to my new studio:

Sew Cool Cam

Of course, by the time I paid for the building and everything else, I didn't have the money for signage, so above the door, it still said *Regal Boutiques*, but in my heart, it was *Sew Cool Cam.*

Unfortunately, as I turned the key, jostling everything around, my fabric slid out of my grip, hitting the ground in heavy thunks and thuds and kicking up a cloud of dust. In a panic, I set my machine on the ground, gathered up the fabric, and hastily wiped it down. Thankfully, most of the dirt came away cleanly, and after a deep breath to unsuccessfully calm my shaking hands and arms, I gathered everything back up and pushed open the door.

The front display area was clean, though bare. Some battered clothing racks were pushed together on the far right side. The main counter, where the cash register would be placed, was perfectly centered, allowing me to greet people as soon as they walked in. To the left were shelves and peg boards stacked on top of each other, and though I had no idea how to hang them, I could already imagine what they might look like on various walls around the front end.

But all of this was for a later time. Where I really wanted to be was in the room in the back, separated by a door behind the counter. I scurried across the floor, the sound of my footsteps reverberating around the empty room. As soon as I neared the counter, I set everything down on its surface and went right for the door.

The knob was heavy and metal, cold as I took it in my hand. My body was quivering uncontrollably as I turned it, anticipating that my dreams would come true on the other side. It wasn't quite as climactic as I had hoped. I pushed the door inside and revealed a room almost as empty as the shop floor, except for several tables that filled the main floor and shelves lining the back wall.

This was going to be my work area. For a year, I had been stuck in my studio apartment, often on the floor of my bathroom or kitchen area, cutting up fabric and then sewing it together with my machine on my kitchen table. My fabric and packing materials were scattered across my living area, spilling out of my only closet and covering my kitchen counter. Now, I had more space than I knew what to do with. It was almost unnerving to have so many choices.

Stepping into the empty space, I tried to imagine where I would place things, where I would pack orders, and what I would eventually buy to fill in the different areas and optimize my workspace.

I was jittery, flitting about from table to table, running my hands along their surfaces, trembling with excitement and nerves.

Unable to control myself, I stretched my arms outward, turning my face toward the ceiling, beyond pleased that I could neither touch either wall nor touch the ceiling. It was space. It was freedom. It was my future. I wanted to laugh with all of my joy when a sudden, unfamiliar sound rang out.

It was a loud, rhythmic beeping. A grating sound that sapped all of the joyous, comforting feeling from the air. It took a few seconds to realize what it was.

My new business phone. As part of the deal with the landlord, he offered to pay for the first few months of the phone contract, which had been put in and left behind by the former tenant. I was more than happy to work from my personal phone, but having a landline felt like an essential step in transitioning from a profitable hobby to a profitable business, so I was excited to have it.

The only problem was that, peering around the room, I didn't see it.

Stomping around the room, the sound got louder as I neared the back wall shelving. After rearranging some boxes that had been left behind, the phone in its cradle was perched at the far right side of the shelf, a rather inconvenient spot that I decided to move soon after this.

With that in mind, I picked up the phone, pressed 'Talk,' and held it to my ear.

Unfortunately, my first word came out in a garbled voice, all of the nerves I had built up strangling me:

"H-hello?"

There was silence on the other side. I was just about to say 'hello' again when, finally, there was light static, presumably from someone on the other end shifting the phone around. A deep, gravelly voice then followed it:

"Hello. Is this *Regal Boutiques*?"

It was so deep and warm that it settled over all of my nervous energy like a balm. I could hardly be upset hearing the former business name from it. There was no telling how long I stood there in silence before the person on the other end asked:

"Hello?"

I shook my head, burning with embarrassment, before responding.

"I'm sorry! No, this is now *Sew Cool Cam*."

The man on the other end fell silent again, and though I couldn't see his reaction, I thought I could feel the disappointment radiating from the other end. Regret ballooned in the pit of my stomach as I awkwardly shifted my weight back and forth between my feet until, finally, my suffering ended.

"'Sew'... Like s-e-w?"

Swallowing, I choked out:

"Y-yes."

"So I assume you are a tailor or something like that? Do you offer tailoring services?"

The rise and fall only to rise again of emotions was making me dizzy, but I followed this wave up all the same, excitedly crying out:

"We do!"

To my surprise, what followed was a heady laugh, resonant and full in its sound. It was so deep that the phone seemed to vibrate against my ear, leaving me ticklish all over.

"Great. Thank goodness. Mary-Ann was great, but I knew she was ready to retire. Speaking of which, what's your name?"

Inexplicably shy, I answered in a hushed tone:

"Cameron. I'm the owner."

He laughed again, causing my cheeks to burn.

"Cameron, it's nice to meet you." He cleared his throat, his light tone suddenly settling into something more serious and straightforward. "I used to get my suits tailored there quite often. Would you be willing to do that for me?"

I silently sent my praises and worship to the signage out front. Thanks to them, I already had my first client for my physical location.

"Of course, sir. I'd be happy to."

I thought I heard a clap on the other end, followed quickly by a curt:

"Excellent." Then, in quick succession, he continued: "I travel pretty frequently and am usually in business meetings during usual business hours, so I can't come in for alterations and fittings."

I froze. How could I pin things and prepare a piece for alteration if I didn't have the person there to do it? Before I could even ask, he continued:

"I'll have it pre-pinned, marked, and delivered to your shop. I'm not strict on deadlines, but, of course, the sooner, the better. My proxy will pick it up. What time do you open?"

Flustered, I sprinted around the room, opening drawers beneath the tables until I found leftover pads of paper and some pens. Snatching out a set, I began to scribble down all of these requirements and expectations. Sweat was already soaking into the pits of my shirt.

Only once I was sure I had everything written down did I shakily respond:

"9:00 am."

He groaned, sending goosebumps racing across my arms.

"Would you be able to meet him at 8:30 AM?"

I thought running my own business meant I could decide when I worked, but with this grumbly man in my ear, I felt compelled to do as he said. Nodding along to myself, I scribbled the time down and circled it.

"That shouldn't be a problem."

"Excellent. Before I let you go, do you take custom requests? Ties, for example?"

I held the pen over the following line, frozen. Ties? What did a busy man like this need custom ties for? I could imagine he probably had a whole collection of expensive, name-brand luxury ties and other accessories already.

Of course, I had made ties before, though, for costumes, as opposed to proper working-man ties. The image of a broad-shouldered businessman in a $10,000 suit with a red and white polka-dot tie, created by me, made me want to sob. I didn't feel cut out for such a task. But as I looked around my empty workshop, waiting to be filled with other employees, more machines, and the like, the idea of someone in the business world wearing one of my ties, possibly recommending my work to others like a walking, talking billboard, was too good to pass up.

Clearing my throat and steadying my heart, I tried to manifest all the confidence buried deep in the pit of my stomach.

"Of course. Would you like to put in an order?"

Without missing a beat, he responded:

"Excellent. Dark, rich colors. Silk, if you have it. I prefer unique patterns over solids. 58 inches in length."

My hand was shaking, the pen sliding around in my grip from my sweat. The words were coming out more like Wingdings and scribbles than anything legible, but my mind was working surprisingly quickly and clearly. I could see a shadow of hands, manly and large, a set of hands that matched the voice dictating his order to me over the phone. He tightened the knot of a wine-colored tie at the base of his neck, then ran his fingers down the front of his tie, letting the amber-colored leaf pattern catch the light.

I wanted to make such a thing for such a man — for this man I didn't know, see, or could imagine.

Choking back a squeal of excitement, I asked:

"How many would you like?"

He chuckled; it sounded like thick honey pooling over my head.

"As many as you can make, and whatever you're planning on charging, triple it for the trouble. I'll add a tip on at the end if you dare charge less."

The threat was playful and kind, but it still sent chills racing down my spine. It was a strange mix of nervous sweats, terrified chills, and comforting, unfamiliar heat. All of these sensations were making me nauseous.

Still, I laughed.

"And what if I charge you an arm or a leg?"

The caller was silent for a while, leaving me squirming as I realized I might have offended him, only to be settled as he murmured:

"I'll give you both, then."

I swallowed, my heart thumping heavily in my chest. With a shaky breath, I asked:

"What name should I put down for this?"

"Clifton Becker."

I scribbled it down, spelling it with two 'f's at first, then marking it out and writing it with one the next time. I liked the way the second version looked better. I was just about to ask him to confirm when he jumped in.

"But *you* can call me Cliff."

I thought there might have been a slight emphasis on the 'you,' sending my heart fluttering. I dropped my pen, leaving a long, squiggly mark across the page. While I tried to get myself together, Mr. Becker continued.

"I don't have any new pieces to be tailored currently, but I have some coming in from Italy tomorrow that may need work. I'll let you know when they arrive so that you can expect my proxy. Do you need anything else?"

I was nodding along, silent, though he couldn't see my reaction. After some time had passed, me needlessly bobbing my head, he asked:

"Cameron?"

A chill shook my entire body. Hearing my name reverberate through the phone and tickle my inner ear was euphoric. His voice was thick and rich like molasses. Something about it massaged me from the inside out, leaving my muscles soft and pliable. The only reason I hadn't melted into a heap on the floor was the table, which I leaned against.

It took far too much effort to choke out a response:

"That sounds just fine, Mr. Becker."

He chuckled, sending another wave of pleasure coursing through my sensitive insides.

"Great. I'll call again about my tie commission. I look forward to speaking with you next time, Cameron."

And just like that, the other end of the phone went dead, leaving me panting and wanting. I set the phone back into the cradle before shifting my attention to the front of my pants, awkwardly distended from my throbbing member. I wanted nothing more than to touch it, though doing so felt a bit blasphemous in the sanctity of my workshop.

But it was *my* workshop.

I was just about to satisfy my needs, pleased with my own excuse, when my stomach gurgled.

Instantly, my lust evaporated. With a sigh, I pulled out my phone, prepared to have something delivered so I could begin working on my first customer's request. But, after checking the banking app on my phone, I found that the balance wasn't sufficient for delivery. It wasn't even enough for pickup.

The day already felt like it was over.

I had brought in all of my materials, and I somehow received a new client, which in turn led to plenty of work. My entire body ached from nerves and the beating I had taken at the gym, and I was compelled to head home, make myself a sandwich, and then head to bed, so that I could start fresh the next day.

After a bit of mental back and forth, with my stomach wailing all the while, I ultimately decided to leave for the day, satisfied with most of the happenings. But as soon as I locked my front door and started toward the bus stop so I could get home, I was once again disturbed by my lack of material.

I didn't want to give up Mr. Becker as a client, but if I couldn't complete his commissions effectively, what would be the point of disappointing him in the end when I could just cancel ahead of time? Yet, recalling his voice and the way it moved me so, I selfishly felt I couldn't give him up, whether it be a professional mistake or otherwise. There would be other clients.

But there would probably never be another like Mr. Becker.

~*~

That night, as I curled up in bed, I took out my phone and went right to my browser, opening an incognito window. It was like second nature, mindlessly going to *PornyPeople.com*, heading to the gay category, and searching through the audio roleplays. They often called them ASMR, but most were anything but. Scanning through the most recent uploads, I found one titled 'Whimpering and Moaning for Your Cock | Femboy ASMR' and queued it up just before sliding on my headphones.

Regular, visual porn was fine, but what really did it for me was the audio. Nothing could beat a good voice.

As expected, as it started, the 'femboy' in question came through squealy and whiny, with slick, wet sounds slipping between his words to fill the empty space. My eyes slid shut while my hand made its way into the front of my underwear, grasping my steadily swelling cock.

I tried to picture them, this small, whiny man, drooling and whimpering with his legs spread wide, stroking his laughably small dick.

"Hngh, I want it. Put it in, please."

But no matter how vigorously I stroked, my penis remained semi-limp in my grip.

Usually, this would've been plenty to get me going, but there was something about this voice and the person in my mind's eye that just wasn't doing it for me. None of my usual tingles and twinges were coming through, no matter how loudly the person cried into my ears.

"My hole is nice and wet. Please put it in."

Groaning, I opened my eyes, shutting off the video while I angrily shook my limp dick.

I was already sexually frustrated from my phone call with my new client, Mr. Becker, whose voice was so weighty and deep it transcended all others. Recalling now, without the stress of my new business looming all around me, I could fully appreciate it. It dipped deep into the pit of my abdomen, resting there, reverberating from the inside out. It was as if my body had turned into an open cavern, filling me with sound that echoed endlessly from wall to wall, ceiling to floor, and every space in between.

It made me feel full.

It made me feel whole.

It made me so goddamn horny.

It was then I realized my useless, flaccid member had suddenly come to life, straining against my fist and pulsing in my palm.

In a flurry, not wanting to waste this moment, I replayed the video.

Once more, that nasally, high-pitched voice came through, but even with it coursing through my ears, it couldn't penetrate my imagination. I took the words and gave them to the voice I craved instead, and rather than imagining that lithe body, I tried to picture that of Mr. Becker.

A man with such a voice was probably equally as heavy. He probably had thick fingers, thick arms, and thick legs. His face was still a mystery, a nebulous shadow on top of this hazy form I was creating. I didn't really care about what he looked like.

All I needed was that voice, which whimpered:

"I can't fuck anyone with this small cock. I need *you* to fuck me."

I nearly laughed. This large man I had created suddenly spread before me with a diminutive cock.

I didn't think, based on his status and tone, that he would be one to beg to be fucked, but this unforeseen situation was all the more alluring.

"Please put it in me."

That simpering tone was too much to bear. In that deep resonance that filled me so deeply, I felt as if I was sinking into my mattress. To hear him begging for me to fuck him — I couldn't hold back. As soon as I went to stroke down my shaft, my cock pulsed once before shooting thick strings of cum up and over my abdomen. I continued to stroke, twitching and jumping from the electric overstimulation as I was still racked with orgasm. I steadily milked out every drop of cum left within my straining balls.

By the time I was done, I expected the lonely emptiness of my chest and abdomen to follow, but as I lay in the afterglow, I found myself full of warmth. That voice was still lingering in the recesses of my brain and the cavern of my body, murmuring in a deep, booming whisper:

"Cameron?"

It was the perfect lullaby to draw me into a state of unconsciousness.

It was a pleasant rest, though waking up covered in dried cum, a soft cock squeezed in my hand, and a yelping and whining pornstar in my ear wasn't ideal. Still, after getting all cleaned up, showered, and dressed, I once again felt that heated fullness.

I was more than ready to get the object of my lustful obsession's ties done.

The thought of hearing his praise reverberating in my ear was all too alluring.

CHAPTER TWO

The following afternoon, I was back in my workshop, preparing to do what I could to meet Mr. Becker's expectations.

The building was cold, as I had neglected to turn on the heat the previous day during all the buzz and excitement. Thankfully, I had brought an oversized sweater with me to wear while I worked. So, as I slipped the thick and heavy knit sweater over my head, a surge of determination and readiness washed over me. The back room, clearly designed for multiple employees, appeared vast and overwhelming. Yet, my humble collection of pins, a single sewing machine, a couple of bolts of fabric, and the landline phone I had just moved, along with my wallet and keys, stood as a testament to my unwavering resolve. They were placed on the end of a table, closest to the entrance, as if to say:

I am here, ready to conquer.

A mild sense of embarrassment washed over me as I surveyed the distance I had yet to cover. However, as I settled in, my mind buzzing with ideas for the store, its products, and its customers, I couldn't help but feel immense excitement. I pushed the sleeves of my sweater up over my elbows, ignoring how they slid back down as soon as I moved to sift through my fabric.

He wanted dark colors. That wine color was still at the forefront of my mind, but looking over what I had on hand, I realized I really didn't have anything even remotely close to what he had requested. There was a single bolt of silk, but it was a light blue, solid color. What I did have in a dark shade had a pattern of bunnies and carrots across it, intended for children-sized pieces, though part of me did wonder what he might say if I did present such a piece to him.

It was all rather depressing.

I glanced down at the yellow notepad on which I had scribbled the order, sad that I hadn't thought to buy something more official for noting orders or printing invoices. He had told me to triple whatever I wanted to charge, but with what I had, I'd charge him nothing, and zero times three was still zero. Deflated, I was tempted to call him back and cancel until I could gather more material, but just as I was bemoaning my poor selection, the phone, resting in its chunky plastic cradle, began to ring.

Part of me hoped it wasn't a new client, as I wasn't sure I'd have the means to complete another custom order. Yet, at the same time, the anticipation of more clientèle excited me — like proof I was succeeding. I picked up the phone, took a moment to clear my throat, and then clicked the 'Talk' key before holding it to my ear.

"Hello, *Sew Cool Cam*, this is Cameron."

There was a familiar, resonant intake of breath. What followed could only be described as a sip of hot tea, warming me from the inside out.

"Cameron. Hi."

It was Clifton. I felt a twinge of guilt in my chest as I glanced at my poor collection of fabrics, and I responded rather stiffly.

"Hello, Mr. Becker. How can I help you?"

His tone was clipped as if he was giving a command, though the words didn't convey the same.

"My friends call me Cliff."

Goosebumps lit across my arms as I imagined what it might be like to be commanded by such an intimidating-sounding man.

"That's nice."

The man laughed so hard and loud that he was gasping for a while afterward. My face burned, unsure of what I had done to garner such a reaction. After collecting himself and audibly swallowing, he clarified:

"Call me Cliff. Not Mr. Becker."

Squirming in my seat, I murmured:

"Alright. You call me Cam, then."

Immediately, he sang:

"Cam."

That bright and playful tone enveloped me in warmth. Once again, I was compelled to touch myself to his voice. I squeezed my free hand into a fist, desperately fighting the urge. Mr. Becker was my one and only big client. If I got hard every time I spoke to him, I doubted he would be my client for very long. It was a relief that we were limited to phone interactions.

Thankfully, while I fought with myself, Mr. Becker carried on.

"I'm rather embarrassed, Cam. You're a brand new business, right?"

I winced, once again reminded how incapable I was of running a business — even a small one. At this point, my heart was sinking into my stomach, anticipating that Mr. Becker had come to his senses and decided he needed someone with more experience and background to do the work he needed. It hurt to imagine he might cancel his commission with me, but I understood it.

Admittedly, it hurt a tad bit more to realize I might never hear his voice again.

But just when I was formulating my response to his inevitable cancellation, something polite and understanding, he threw me for a loop entirely:

"I'm so sorry, Cam. I should've paid you a deposit for the work ahead of time."

I blinked, my mouth moving without sound. I had been so sure where this conversation was going, so to have it seemingly going in the opposite direction was breaking my brain. All I could manage to stammer out was:

"I'm sorry?"

There was another one of those deep chuckles that sent shivers racing down my spine.

"Cam, if ever someone comes wanting something custom from you, take a deposit. You can use that to replenish your stock, have a buffer if they decide to back out, and it's just more in your favor." I felt like I needed my notepad again, but before I could go hunting for it, he carried on: "For your custom work, you should also really set up some kind of contract. I know some lawyers you could speak to and get a draft started. You can't be too trusting when you get into business."

It was funny that someone who was clearly a businessman in his own right was warning me about doing business. He was a bad example of an untrustworthy customer. Still, I took his words to heart, bobbing my head along to his words like he could see my reaction.

Finally, he asked:

"Do you have a preferred app we can use so I can transfer the funds?"

I fumbled with my phone, my hands shaking from

nerves I couldn't explain. I flipped through the various apps on my phone until I pulled up my finance app. With it open, I gave Cliff the info needed for a transfer, and within moments, I received a notification.

Clicking it open, I nearly dropped my phone.

An extra $2,000 sat in my app, ready to be transferred to my business account.

"D-did you mean to send me $2,000?"

My voice was shaking so badly that I was sure Cliff probably didn't understand a word I was saying. But I was still too stunned to ask again.

There was no way this man thought $2,000 was a deposit. Just how many ties was he expecting me to make?

But to my surprise, his answer to my questioning tone was shock and... embarrassment?

"Was that not enough? How much more do you need? Just give me a number."

I spluttered. My brain was spinning. I was simultaneously thinking of all the fabric I could buy with that sum and wondering how a man could possibly think $2,000 was too little of a deposit.

"No, no! This is fine!"

Cliff hummed.

"Great. One more lesson before I go. If someone tells you they're willing to give you more, take more." He chuckled then. "You don't have to be cutthroat. But you should always put yourself in the best position whenever possible. It's better for your business starting out, and you'll probably be able to put out a better product."

Though I knew little to nothing about this man, hearing his jovial tone over the phone was a great relief from the anxiety and worry I had been entrenched in not long before. I nodded along to his words, agreeing with him, even though, once again, I realized he couldn't see me.

There was more of that deep but soft laughter, tickling my inner ear and cottony gray matter. Chills were racing down my spine, and I did everything I could to not let out a moan that was sitting heavily in my chest. Thankfully, I didn't have to hold myself back for long as Cliff cleared his throat.

"Sorry for the trouble, Cam. I've got to go. I look forward to seeing what you end up making."

And without waiting for my response, the line went dead.

With a shaking hand, I pulled the phone away from my face and stared at it in disbelief. Yet, looking into the app again, there was no doubt. The money was there. I set the phone back into its cradle and then slouched back into my seat. My heart was still pounding so hard and loud that I was getting dizzy.

If he thought $2,000 was a deposit, I would probably be making ties for him for the rest of his life for whatever sum he imagined the final total to be. Once again, the image of that made-up beefy body without a face came to mind, and the prospect of being tied to it and dressing it for the rest of my life didn't seem too bad.

My thighs quivered, leaving me sighing deeply.

I didn't have to look or feel it to know my cock was rock hard. This really was becoming a problem. Just as I was reaching down to give in to my lust, the sound of my storefront doorbell ringing left me scrambling up instead.

I called out, "Coming!" while adjusting my cock so hopefully it wasn't too apparent before scuttling out of the workroom, the $2,000 and how I would spend it now dancing around in the forefront of my mind.

~*~

I loved sewing, cutting fabric, and working with my hands to create something from scratch. But I had to admit that nothing was more fun than shopping for new fabric. I could make a dozen new pieces, but no high could compare to the high I got when I bought new material to work with. It was truly a problem.

Back when I had a day job that I could use to fund my side gig, I often spent weekends visiting various craft and fabric stores, hunting for unique patterns, and filling my small apartment with bolts and bolts of pretty fabric that I'd sometimes just admire. I would imagine all kinds of uses for it, but I was too scared to use it, worrying that I'd ruin my most expensive and unique selections. Since starting as a full-time tailor, those visits had been significantly limited to just what was needed to complete a project, and not much else. As a result, those more unique fabric purchases quickly became an eyesore.

I was also often limited to online shopping, which wasn't nearly as exciting or fulfilling. The amount of fabric sitting forlorn in my online shopping cart was pitiful.

But with Mr. Becker's money burning a hole in my bank account, I was compelled to finally take my online shopping cart, like a virtual shopping list, to my local craft store. So, the very next day, after an evening of panic sketching in my workroom, I made my way to the store — business credit card in hand. I still couldn't believe I had $2,000 to spend as I liked. Even as I entered the store and grabbed a cart, I found myself double- and triple-checking the balance I had transferred into my business bank account.

Just as it had been every other time I checked, there was, in fact, $2,000 still there.

Finally, reassured now that I was in the store, I could bask in the atmosphere I had missed.

Immediately, I was hit with the astringent scent of new

linen and floor cleaner. It sent chills racing down my spine as I meandered down one of the many aisles. It was pretty early in the day, so other than the man at the cash register ignoring my presence, I seemed to be the only person inside. Without the pressure of other patrons, I took my sweet time, going up and down the aisles. I fully intended, with this budget, to use silks for the project, but I still went down the other aisles, admiring the various patterns in the cotton, the affordable pricing in the polyester, and the like.

Admittedly, by the time I reached the silk, I had a healthy pile of other fabrics in my basket.

Once again, I checked my business account and found that the $2,000 hadn't evaporated into thin air.

But then I caught sight of the time.

It was amazing how long it had taken to get here, as it was nearing lunchtime. Unsurprisingly, the sounds of the store were growing. The front doors were sliding open and closed more frequently, and the noise of screeching buggy wheels along the floor filled the once-peaceful serenity of the empty store. As voices neared my area, I felt pressured to pick out everything I needed to check out and return to my own store. I still hadn't figured out what my hours should be, but hearing so many people milling about in public now, I was compelled to get back to open up for my own prospective customers.

Cursing my nonchalant time-wasting earlier, I sped down the silk aisle, glancing at all of the various colors and patterns.

Now that I was actually looking at them, I realized I had no idea what my client, Mr. Becker, would enjoy. Did he like cool tones or warm tones? Was he a fan of patterns or solids? I wasn't even sure what vests, shirts, and jackets he had to wear with them. At the very least, I wished I knew what he looked like so I could choose based on that, but even that was a mystery to me.

I was back to meandering, stumped. Some garish paisley patterns, with vibrant purple and pink, were unquestionably loud and eye-catching. I pressed the fabric between my fingers, admiring how the silk caught the light. Was Mr. Becker the type of person who would like something so forward and bright?

I couldn't help imagining a faceless man with a large chest. Ties always looked best on large chests. He had a white collared shirt, the buttons straining to keep his massive pecs covered. A pair of heavy hands with thick fingers reached up, straightening the bare collar.

I tried to picture a purple and pink paisley tie tied around his neck. The faceless man tightened the knot with one hand, running his other down the blade of the tie, presumably slipping the tail into the tail loop in the back. The design was loud and proud, taking some of the focus away from his ample chest, which I found disappointing.

In a tantalizing fashion, he snatched the tie off, carelessly undoing the knot and clenching the limp thing between his hands. He looked like he was threatening to tie someone up with it, but I couldn't help imagining it wrapped around his wrists instead.

In that deep, sultry voice, the only thing I knew of Cliff Becker, he begged:

Tie me up.

It was in the middle of my perverted musing that someone murmured:

"Excuse me."

Shocked back into reality, I stepped forward, yanking my cart along with me to make room for a young woman who was ambling down the aisle with various bolts of fabric in her arms. I blinked, shifting my gaze between the fabric pinched between my fingertips and the woman who was glancing back at me, her brows furrowed in a mixture of confusion and concern. Thoroughly embarrassed, I dropped the fabric as if it had burned me and ignored the paisley patterns entirely, going for solids and some subtle polka dots. I did grab some brighter colors, but kept the rest pretty plain.

I was just about to race out of the aisle when a wine-colored fabric with gold floral patterns racing across it caught my eye. It wasn't pink and purple paisley, but it wasn't a boring solid or polka dot. It was refined, something I thought Cliff Becker might be. Swallowing, I grabbed a bolt of it, adding it to the pile in my basket.

My face burned as I barreled through the aisles, sweating as I waited at the cutting table, before ambling back up to the cash register, hoping no one else had witnessed my awkward display. On the way, I picked up some wool inserts for the ties' cores. All the while, my heart had fallen into the pit of my stomach, leaving me feeling heavy and sick while my chest was light. My cock, however, was throbbing painfully in the front of my pants.

CHAPTER THREE

After stopping for lunch and shipping some finished online orders, the sun was well below the horizon by the time I made it back to my workshop. To my surprise, a note was shoved into the gap between my front door and the frame, which I found to be someone's phone number and a request to call them regarding some repair inquiries. I cursed myself, determined to come up with some standard hours, as I unlocked the door and made my way inside. After a moment of musing, I locked the door back behind me. I had already missed out on a full day of work, and though Mr. Becker hadn't given me a deadline or any expectation of how many pieces he wanted, I felt compelled to start as soon as possible. So, even though it was well after what I'd just decided were my shop hours, I sat myself down in my workshop, various fabrics laid out before me, and I mused once more.

Once again, I was struck with uncertainty. If only I could've sent Mr. Becker pictures of the fabric so he could give me some idea of whether they were to his taste or not, this wouldn't be such a difficult decision. I pondered whether it was worthwhile to buy a computer for the shop so I could communicate more effectively and possibly send pictures via email to my customers. Then, my landline rang. Clearing my throat, I picked it up:

"*Sew Cool Cam.*"

A deep baritone sent vibrations through my inner ear and tickled my brain, conjuring my fantasies from the fabric store earlier.

"Cam. Good afternoon."

With a shaking breath, I tried to push my perversions out of my mind as I responded.

"Cliff, how are you?"

There was a rumbling chuckle coursing through me from the other side of the phone. Like a switch, the soft cock in my pants was twitching to life. Once again, the image of that big, broad, faceless man returned to the forefront of my mind. I tugged at the front of my pants, giving my throbbing cock some room to grow while Cliff's deep laughter waned.

"I'm doing very well, Cam. Thanks for asking." There was the sound of papers shuffling. Although my workshop was windowless, I knew it had to be pitch-black outside. I felt some kinship with Cliff, knowing we were both working well into the night. "I'm surprised I caught you. I figured you'd be off work."

Clearing my throat, I did my best to keep my hands busy with the various fabrics I had chosen. I naturally reached for the wine-colored fabric, admiring the way the gold shifted in the light.

"I'm surprised you called. Are you still working this late in the evening?"

Cliff chuckled. He laughed a lot more than I anticipated a businessman might.

"When I'm traveling, work is never done." Again, there was the soft, shuffling sound of papers being moved, followed by light tapping, as if he were straightening them up in a pile. "Speaking of work, I wanted to check and see when I could expect my first tie."

My heart was about to fall out of my butt, and the boner I had been so desperately trying to coax away deflated instantly. Unsure of what to say, I started to stutter. Again, Cliff's laughter cut through the tension.

"No pressure, Cam. I'll take them as they come." But even as he started with that, he hummed. "*But...* I have a meeting coming up. I'd love something nice to wear to it."

I swallowed, nervous but emboldened.

"When's the meeting?"

There was more humming as if he wasn't exactly sure. Then, he responded:

"Wednesday at noon."

That was two days from now. It was tight, especially when other work was steadily pouring in, and I still had many other errands to run to really get my business going. But it wasn't impossible.

I was growing confident. Finally.

But Cliff's voice came through the phone, sympathetic and gentle as he said:

"If you can't, it's not a problem. I'll just—"

Reflexively, I jumped right out of my seat, hitting the table with my knees and inadvertently causing my fabric and various tools to fall to the floor. I winced but refrained from crying out, choking instead as I croaked:

"No, no. I can do it."

There was silence, soon followed by more of that surprising laughter.

"Excellent. I'm looking forward to seeing it."

My knees ached from where they hit the table as I knelt down to collect everything that fell off the table. Once again, my eyes fell on that wine-colored fabric with the gold floral pattern. I pursed my lips.

"Can I ask you something, Mr. Becker?"

"Of course. It must be serious if you're back to calling me Mr. Becker."

Now I was chuckling, though my throat was constricting.

"Yes, sir. Um... how do you feel about colors and patterns?"

Suddenly, his voice was distant, and I could hear him talking to someone else, but I couldn't be sure who. Once he was speaking to me again, his voice was lower and somehow deeper. It sent chills through my entire body as that husky, hushed sound coursed through my head and permeated my whole being.

"I love them. The bolder, the better." There was more talking between him and someone else. Then, he continued. "I'm sorry, Cam. I have to go. I'll call you back tomorrow."

And just like that, the line went dead.

I was left standing there, clutching the fabric I would use for his first tie in one hand, the other falling to my side with the silent phone. Meanwhile, my cock was back to standing up and proud, throbbing as I recalled that voice saying the words:

I love them.

I knew he was talking about patterns and colors, but I couldn't help imagining him talking about my fingers, my hands, my nuts, and the like while I did all manner of things to the hulking body I conjured in my mind's eye. As soon as I locked up and headed home to my apartment, the only thing on my mind was my faceless paramour, telling me how much he loved all of my various parts as I used them on him.

~*~

Once again, I was in bed, trying to find the perfect audio porn to finally satisfy my desires for Cliff Becker, but no matter what I played, nothing rivaled the sound of his voice, stroking me from the inside out. But every voice was either too bright and whiny or so put on that it was painful to listen to. Each time I started a new video, I found myself stroking a dick stuck between falling limp and twitching to full hardness.

It was maddening.

In frustration, I took out my earbuds and set my phone down on my side table. In the silence, all I could do was stare down at my member, pitifully flopped up onto my stomach. I groaned, giving it a light tap, which jolted it up but did little else.

But just as I was about to tuck it back in place and turn for the night, that voice echoed in my head.

I love them.

Finally, my cock sprang to life, and the image of my faceless patron bloomed at the forefront of my mind. This faceless man was kneeling before me, his tongue swiping at the underside of my balls. The feeling of that light pressure on such a sensitive place was dangerous and threatening, but it only made me want more.

I grasped the faceless man's hair and tugged it back, staring into his blank face and trying to imagine what features he might have. I tried facial hair. I tried blue eyes and brown hair. I tried brown eyes with blond. But it all faded into a smudged amalgam, except for his mouth, which held a tongue that lolled out of the corner.

The corners of his open lips turned up into a grin, carrying with it that deep chuckle I often heard radiating from the other side of the phone.

"Do you want to fuck my mouth or fuck these?"

27

As he spoke, his hands worked the front of his shirt, opening up the top to reveal ample pecs. They appeared firm and muscled, but as his fingers pressed into them, they easily gave way, delicate and soft like marshmallows. I was positively salivating.

Like an animal, I dropped down on top of him, pushing his body down onto the floor and pinning him beneath me. I grabbed the remainder of his buttoned shirt and ripped it open, finding immense satisfaction in the way the buttons scattered around the room of my mind.

He laughed, his hands pressing into either side of his chest, pushing the thick mounds together until there was at least a small bit of cleavage for my cock to slide into. They were lovely and smooth, and as I pressed my knees onto either side of his ribs, they only became all the more alluring as he spat onto them. Using his thick fingers, he swiped the saliva across each mound, then, holding two fingers together, slid them in and out of his cleavage.

In that deep, heady baritone, he purred:

"They're ready for you."

My dick couldn't be any harder. Grabbing the base of it, I pressed the head just beneath the crease between his breasts. I wanted to take my time and enjoy him, but feeling the warmth of his skin and seeing the shimmer of his moistened flesh, I couldn't control myself. I thrust upward, the force pushing against and separating his breasts, so I could clearly see my cock sliding between them. As the tip of my dick neared his face, he knelt upward, kissing and licking it until my swollen and throbbing head was shimmering as much as his breasts.

My body was quaking from all of the stimuli.

The warm and firm pressure from the breasts squeezing my shaft, the velvety moisture of his mouth teasing my tip, and then the rhythmic slapping of my balls against his body was just too much.

The coiling heat in the pit of my stomach was drawing up the muscles in my thighs until I couldn't hold back anymore. Crying out Cliff's name, I came, shooting hot, sticky cum across his neck, chin, and face. His tongue flickered out, swiping a thick stripe off his chin. He purred like it was a fine meal, which he punctuated with a grumbling:

"Delicious."

But my lusty imaginings were fading away as my balls steadily emptied.

Once I was done, I found myself jolted back to reality, staring down at my bedding. I blinked, shocked to discover that I had indeed cum on some pillowy softness — my pillows, to be exact. Half disgusted, half disappointed, and… well, I guess a third would be more accurate, with the last third dedicated to satisfied. I picked up my soiled pillow and tossed it off the bed to be dealt with in the morning.

Thoroughly worn out, I tucked my member back into my pants, slipped beneath the covers, and fell asleep before I could even begin to feel guilt over masturbating to my imagined version of Cliff Becker.

CHAPTER FOUR

The next morning, I found that I could no longer avoid what I had done the night before. I was bombarded by embarrassment and attraction, wanting to do it again while also swearing I never would. As I brushed my teeth, I mused over my muscled faceless man, but as I washed out my mouth, I couldn't even face myself in the mirror. I was a walking contradiction, a pendulum swinging back and forth from lust to shame.

And this constant whiplash back and forth wouldn't stop until I made it to work, unlocked my shop, and made my way inside — though it didn't stop by my choice or effort.

Instantly, I was struck by how cold it was. There was no difference between the outside temperature and the inside temperature. A distraction was welcome, but this was not the one I would've picked. Bemoaning my poor luck, I shuffled to the workshop area and fiddled with my thermostat. As expected, no matter what I did, the heat wouldn't kick on. Frustrated, I sighed, and like it was mocking me, my breath hung white in the air before dissipating, making me shiver all the more.

Though it had been working perfectly fine the day before, my heat had gone out. I wasn't sure if it was due to running it all night or something else, but it was a pain in the ass all the same. Once again, I was thankful I had brought my sweater with me, but even that wasn't enough now, as winter loomed ahead, chilling the inside of buildings when there was no heat to combat it.

Before I settled down at my workstation, I texted my landlord, hoping for an instant reply, but received none. That wasn't surprising. It was fairly early in the day, since I was trying to establish a 9:00 AM opening time, like I had told Mr. Becker to begin with. Still, this felt like one more bad omen, and I nearly decided to close up shop and just go back home to try to avoid it altogether.

But the note with a potential client's phone number was still sitting on my table, beckoning me to call. Similarly, Mr. Becker's request was haunting the back of my mind. I couldn't possibly leave and waste a day, regardless of the bad omens.

So, with a sigh, I took a seat where I had left everything the day before and started to work.

The call went well, leading to some more alteration work. I spent a little bit of time organizing my new fabric and storing it in the built-in storage. Admittedly, a lot of what I was doing was procrastination. While the anxiety of needing to get Mr. Becker's order done burned in the pit of my stomach, the fear of messing it all up was so much stronger.

I had made countless pieces in the past, some for the fun of it and others for actual orders, but Mr. Becker was the biggest client I had ever worked with, so the pressure to make something perfect was all-encompassing.

I was determined to do it, but I was afraid to try and fail.

But as I finished up all of the busy work I could think of, I was left with only one option: starting Mr. Becker's order. Begrudgingly, I made my way back to my workstation. I had left a few pieces of fabric out to choose from. My eyes were immediately drawn to the wine-colored fabric with the gold pattern, but when compared to the other fabrics I had grabbed, it appeared garish. I had been so sure about it the day before, but now, faced with it, I was questioning myself.

But his words echoed through my brain:

I love them. The bolder, the better.

This was the first tie he'd ever have from me. It would be the only representation of my work he'd have, and I wanted it to be the best. If he liked bold, this was the one. Swallowing back as much of the fear and worry as I could muster, and trusting my instincts, I plucked up the wine-colored fabric and got to work.

Well, 'work' was a generous term.

I tried my best to work, but all my delays and procrastination had wasted most of the day, and what remained of the afternoon was taken up by the few customers who came inside to consult about various tailoring jobs. It was great that people were actually coming in and requesting my services for various things, such as taking in pageant dresses and pinning up long pants, but after spending time on other tasks, I was left panicked over what little time I had left. With the sunlight gone along with my heating, by the time I could sit down to do any significant work, it was freezing in my building.

And what would've been easier a few hours earlier was so much more difficult in the cold of the night.

My hands shook as I tried to line up my pattern along the fabric I had chosen for Mr. Becker's tie. Just as I would line it up to where I wanted the fabric cut, my hands would jerk, throwing it off entirely. Frustrated, I groaned, plopping back down into my work chair and pulling out my smartphone. Glancing at the lock screen, it read *8:32 PM*. Once again, another day was wasted, and I was growing antsy.

Just when I was about to give it another go, the landline began to ring. I stared at the plastic phone, shaking in its cradle while it sang out a tinny, annoying tune. I suspected it was none other than the man who seemed to haunt my life, but I had no way to know for sure. It wasn't until the third ring that I finally picked up the phone, clicked to accept the call, and held it to my ear.

"*Sew Cool Cam*, how may I help you?"

Cliff Becker's voice, deep and heavy, cut through the static of the landline, smooth as ever and sending chills racing down my spine. I was already cold, but he somehow made me shake more. Even more so as his voice carried the sound of my name with it:

"Cam."

It was bright and sing-songy, as if he were excited to hear from a long-lost friend or family member. It surely would make anyone's heart flutter, but maybe mine even more so as memories of his faceless, half-naked form took over my thoughts. I swallowed, shaking my head like that would shake the images out of the forefront of my mind.

Unfortunately, as I tried to respond, I failed to realize how much the cold had affected me. As soon as I opened my mouth, my teeth began to chatter, causing my words to come out shaky and repetitive:

"M-m-mr. B-b-becker."

Embarrassed, I covered my mouth, unsure how to stop myself from sounding like that, but it was too late. Cliff, in a serious and worried tone, asked:

"Cam? Are you alright?"

I shook my head, completely forgetting that he couldn't

see me.

Swallowing, focusing intently on my mouth, I tried my best to keep my teeth and jaw from moving erratically.

"S-sorry. My h-heat is out, so I'm a bit ch-chilly."

I wanted to melt into the floor. Not only would I be warm then, but I could also escape all this embarrassment with my most high-profile client. It was only made worse by how sexually attracted I was to him without ever seeing his face.

But I had to admit, hearing how worried he was over me was mildly satisfying in its own way. I wished it were under different circumstances, but still.

"Your heat is out? How long has it been out?"

Failing to realize this conversation was a bit more personal than our professional relationship warranted, I answered:

"M-maybe overnight. T-this morning at the l-latest."

That deep, thoughtful hum, which was becoming all too familiar, tickled my inner ear.

"Have you reached out to your landlord?" Before I could even respond, he was speaking to someone else, his voice further away than it was before. "Can you get me the number for the landlord of *Sew Cool Cam*? I think I know who owns that area, but I want to make sure." Finally, his voice was close again, "Sorry, Cam. You'll have heat again in the morning."

Dumbfounded, I found myself nodding along like this was all normal when it was anything but. Sometime over the course of this conversation, I found that the cold had faded — at least mentally. Cliff's voice was warm and enveloped me thoroughly. At this rate, I never wanted this phone call to end.

And thankfully, it seemed Cliff wasn't interested in it ending any time soon, either.

He laughed, cutting through the lonely chill in the room.

"Don't take offense to this, Cam, but why are you working in the cold when you could be at home working when the store is closed?"

I blinked.

It hadn't even occurred to me to do such a thing. How long had I been working on the floor of my studio apartment with my bed pushed against the wall to give me more space, scrap fabric scattered all around me? All of a sudden, I had a store and a professional workspace, and I didn't even think to just take my work home with me. With a groan, I slapped my hand over my face, hiding my face and visible embarrassment from no one but myself.

Once again, Cliff's laughter tickled my ear.

"For a savvy young entrepreneur, you're a bit airheaded, aren't you?"

Dragging my hand down to expose my eyes, I glared into the wall.

"I like to think of myself as more of an artist than an entrepreneur, thank you." It then occurred to me that I was talking with a client. So, hastily and awkwardly, I followed it up with a stuttered "… s-sir."

Again, a pleasant and warm giggle.

"No need to be so formal. I quite like the more relaxed and snippy Cam."

While he hadn't said he necessarily liked me, hearing the word 'like' along with my name from someone like Cliff Becker had my heart pounding so hard and fast I felt dizzy. I had to admit that, even from our brief interactions over the phone, I had come to like him quite a bit. He seemed boisterous and extroverted. Paired with his positive energy, wit, and well-spokenness, he was quite a fun conversation partner. Plus, he was counter to everything I was.

What was I thinking? I hardly knew this man, yet here I

was, fantasizing over all of these romantic notions about a complete stranger. It was so unbelievable that I couldn't hold back. Before I knew it, I was cackling, the air coming from my lungs in great white clouds that hung in the room. I had been daydreaming so much that it was fitting for the room to be full of clouds.

By the time I was done, I was wheezing, sucking in sharp, cold air that cut as much as it filled me.

It was so painful it made my eyes well with tears.

As I was wiping them away, coughing, a quiet, heavy whisper cut through the silence on the other end of the line:

"You have a nice laugh, Cam."

Though I was freezing inside, my face was suddenly burning.

Before I could come up with any kind of response, Cliff continued:

"I'm sorry, Cam. I have to go. Get home safe and stay warm. I'll check in again tomorrow. Goodnight."

And with that, the other end went dead. It was a silly thought, but it almost felt like he was desperate to hang up — like he was as nervous as I was. But there was no way that was possible.

Still, I couldn't help replaying his final words to me, and wondering if the almost imperceptible tremble in that 'goodnight' was just my imagination or not. And I continued to wonder long after I had gotten home. Once again, Cliff Becker was the very last thing I thought of before I went to bed and lingered long after I had fallen asleep.

CHAPTER FIVE

Just as he had promised, as I was coming back to the shop the next morning, a work van was already parked out front. After I confirmed who I was and let them inside, the two HVAC specialists wordlessly went to work. Within an hour, I had heat again.

It was a silly, romantic notion, but I couldn't help feeling like Cliff's warmth was embracing me.

I had a few orders to finish up for afternoon pickup, and in between, I had to stop to answer the phone or greet customers who had further inquiries regarding more tailoring requests. So, by the time I was ready to sit down and really focus on Cliff's tie, the store was closed.

But unlike before, I felt ready. So, without hesitation, I started.

Yet, just as I folded over the fabric, lining up my pattern on top of it, the phone rang. I didn't have to look to know who it was. He was the only person who called after hours. I couldn't help wondering what work he might do to need so many neckties and also to be up so late. Clearing my throat, I picked up the phone, accepted the call, then nestled it between my ear and my shoulder before I spoke:

"*Sew Cool Cam,* Cameron speaking."

His voice rumbled out, warm-sounding as always.

"Hello, Cam, my dear tailor."

Although he had always been friendly, this was much more personal. The way he spoke was softer, less precise, as if he were perfectly relaxed. Perhaps he wasn't working late for a change? Every time we'd spoken before, it always seemed like we weren't truly alone. He was always calling out to someone to ask them a question or give them a new task, but I got the sense that right now, for once, he was entirely alone, and something was alluring about being entirely alone with Cliff Becker, even if we were miles and miles apart.

I idly rubbed the fabric of what would eventually be his tie between my fingers, pushing the pattern out of place. It wasn't that big of a deal since I hadn't made any marks yet, but I frowned down at it all the same.

Swallowing, I tried my best to sound as familiar as I could as I responded:

"Ah, yes. My dear customer. What can I do for you tonight?"

"I wanted to check in and make sure we were still good for the tie pickup tomorrow... *and* make sure you weren't freezing to death in that quaint little shop of yours."

As I stared down at the silk in my hands, still not done, I was tempted to ask him for more time, but the image of a tie I had made, hanging between the ample pecs I had conjured in my lusty fantasies before, came to mind. Flushed, I was determined more than ever to have it finished by tomorrow.

"No worries. It will be ready." Clearing my throat, I suddenly felt shy. "And I can't thank you enough for helping with the heat. I'm actually pretty toasty right now."

I could hear him hum, such a rich and relaxed sound. It

was hard to believe this was the same man who had so precisely dictated all of his requirements for these custom pieces not so long ago. Finally, after a characteristic giggle, he responded:

"I must admit. I really had to work hard to come up with a reason to call you because I wanted to hear your voice."

My entire body seemed to lock up, and the soft silk in my hands dropped back onto the table in a heap. My heart, on the contrary, was only speeding up. I coughed, trying to keep my voice level as I responded:

"Oh?"

He chuckled once more, and then there was static. It sounded like he might be shifting the phone or moving around with it pressed against his face. After a while, it finally cleared, and I could just barely make out the sound of gulping.

It was a few seconds longer before it stopped, replaced with a pleasant sigh.

Unable to stand the awkward silence, I cleared my throat and whispered as if someone might be listening.

"Sir?"

He whimpered, and I could just barely hear him grumble:

"Why won't you call me Cliff?"

Before I could respond, he hummed again.

"Tell me, Cam, do you drink?"

Apparently, he did. I tried to imagine what he might be having. With his deep voice, I imagined a large man, but given the 58-inch tie length specifications, he was more than likely average-sized. Either way, I pictured dark liquor, like bourbon, in a short glass.

I swallowed, imagining what the man holding such a glass might look like.

Finally, I responded:

"Not often."

He laughed again before the sound of tinkling glass rang out on his side of the phone.

It was probably something with ice.

"That's probably for the best. You need to stay sharp, working with your hands like you do. You must have lovely hands."

I found myself glancing at my hands, wondering if they really were lovely.

All the while, he continued to muse, seemingly carrying on a conversation with himself.

"I'd like to see your hands."

I swallowed again. There was a distinct tonal shift. What had been lighthearted and silly banter moments before had suddenly settled into something heavy and serious. While he said it as an idle musing, there was an edge of what felt like a command.

I suddenly found myself wanting to prostrate myself before him, hands outstretched, awaiting his judgment.

More shocking than that, there was a nervous swelling at the crotch of my pants.

What had this man done to me?

As if he could see my predicament, he murmured:

"I'd like to see you do all kinds of things with your hands."

Shaking, I tentatively reached down with one hand to grasp the front of my pants, jumping at the stimulation as my hand pressed against my wanting cock. I used my other hand to grab the phone, holding it to my head so I could straighten up and focus intently on the man on the other end.

"What kind of things?"

He breathed in deeply. I could imagine his chest

expanding, a tie I made hanging loosely at the center of his bare chest. Though he was talking about my hands, I couldn't help picturing his instead, reaching down, grasping my pants, and yanking them down.

Imitating it, in reality, was impossible in my current predicament, so I instead fumbled with my zipper, hastily tugging it down, then shoving my hand within my underwear to tug out my ever-hardening member.

He hummed, then sighed, grumbling so deeply his words felt like static as they tickled my ear.

"You're going to think I'm a pervert."

If only he knew what I was doing on the other end of the call. I was the real pervert here.

But I didn't let him know that. Instead, grasping the base of cock, I said:

"I already suspect that you might be with how many late-night calls I get from you."

His deep chuckle tickled my ear, sending waves of shivers down my back. I stroked slowly at first, gradually reaching the head where jolts of pleasure raced down my shaft, leaving me jerking and squeaking in my chair.

I had to suck in my lower lip, chewing on it, just to keep from crying out into the phone.

Cliff grumbled:

"Hard to be a pervert when I've never seen you in person."

It wasn't all that difficult. I was doing just fine at it. Milky cum was beginning to leak out of my tip, my cock pulsing in my hand like it was crying out for more.

I grunted, unable to hold back.

"Try me."

He was silent for a while. So silent, I feared he might hear the slick, wet sound my hand was making as I stroked myself, or, worse yet, that he might hear the little gasps and groans that threatened to slip out between my lips.

Finally, that heavy voice coursed through the phone, massaging my ear canal and gray matter, leaving behind a euphoric tingling.

"I'd love to lick your fingers."

The whole time, I had imagined myself prostrating before him, but this was putting a whole other thought in my mind. I wanted him before me, begging for a chance to just kiss my hands. It was satisfying yet frustrating, as I had no clue what this man I wanted to dominate even looked like.

In this version, he was a shadowy figure with a mask covering the upper part of his face. His mouth was open, waiting and wanting, drool dribbling down one corner in anticipation.

I tilted my head back, groaning, unrelenting, as my hips began to thrust upward, desperate for more stimulation than what my hand could provide.

"There's nothing quite like having a man's fingers shoved into my mouth — prying it open and making me drool."

Cliff continued whispering dirty fantasies and wants right into my ear, and though it was all just sound, it felt just like the rough hand of a man running his hands up and down my body. More specifically, that warm voice was wrapped firmly around my dick, stroking in long, languid pulls.

And like my dick had a puppet string, my entire body moved right along with it, bucking and humping into my hand. And the sound — I was thrusting so hard that the seat beneath me screamed as it scraped along the floor. All the while, I was picturing my masked Cliff, taking the length of the tie around his neck and wrapping it around my shaft. As he stroked, the gold of the fabric glinted in the light, reflecting off his sweat-covered flesh.

Desperate for that sensation in the real world, I knelt forward, fumbling for the piece of fabric I had just been using to make Cliff's tie. Once it was in my wet hand, I pressed it to the engorged head of my penis, jolting as the silk came in contact with my sensitive flesh.

"I have a thing for hands, you know. I was never any good with mine."

Something about that was so attractive. Picturing a successful man like Cliff on his knees, clumsily stroking my cock while he sucked on my fingers, was as cute as it was titillating. I'd shove my fingers in his mouth, enjoy the way his tongue desperately flailed, trying to taste and suck on them, all the while his large hands did their best to stroke me to climax with that vibrant fabric shimmering in the light.

I growled, rubbing the silk back and forth across the head of my cock, the rough, painful friction slowly giving way to pure pleasure as the fabric grew damp with my cum.

I could see his mouth wide open, drooling all over my hands and whimpering, with steaming tears falling from beneath his mask.

As if this version of Cliff could hear me and respond, I found myself grunting:

"Say my name."

And like magic, directly in my ear, Cliff's voice clearly said:

"Cameron."

That was all it took. All I needed to hear was that deep and husky voice saying my name to send all of the pleasure that had been twisting and twisting in the pit of my abdomen to suddenly unwind. My hand shook as I held the soaked silk fabric over the head of my pulsing cock. With what seemed to be never-ending twitches, cum leaked from my tip, steadily coursing down the sides of my shaft.

All the while, I moaned and groaned, enthralled by the deep, raspy breathing coming from the other end of the phone.

Once my orgasm was finally done, and I had enough control of my faculties to be embarrassed by the wet silk stuck to the tip of my dick, Cliff sighed:

"Well, that sounded fun."

It was only then that an inkling of what I was doing, and with whom I was doing it with, invaded my lust-addled brain. Sure, he was presumably buzzed at the minimum and drunk at the maximum, but I was stone-cold sober. While he might have gone along with it, I imagined that when he did sober up, he might not be too pleased with his tailor having phone sex with him, especially when he openly admitted he was attracted to men — or at least their hands.

I didn't necessarily hide my sexual preferences, but I certainly didn't share them with just anyone, and a man of presumably immense power like Cliff Becker probably didn't want that information in the hands of someone like me, either.

I was just beginning to stutter out an apology and a promise of silence when Cliff said:

"I know we just had an intimate phone encounter, but I have to ask: do I make you uncomfortable?"

Staring down at the expensive silk, soaked in cum, sitting on the tip of my soft dick like a misshapen veil, I wasn't sure if he made me any more uncomfortable than I made myself. Still, I had to admit he did make me nervous at least. As if he could read my energy through the phone, Cliff sighed.

"If I do, please feel free to be honest. I'll let you keep the money, and you won't have to work with me anymore."

"Wait! No! You're fine." I had blurted the words out

without thinking, so when silence followed, I wasn't sure what else to say. Swallowing and trying my best to slow my racing heart, I tried to clarify. "I-it's true you do make me *nervous*. But you don't bother me or anything. I enjoyed what we… just did."

Silence followed once more, and with it came more mounting anxiety and embarrassment.

Finally, though, Cliff's laugh enveloped me, settling *most* of my nerves.

"You're honest, Cam. I like that. And I like what we just did, too. I'd like it if we could do some other things in person sometime, too. What do you think?"

I blinked.

Whether it was due to post-nut euphoria or something else altogether, I couldn't fathom what we would do together in person.

"Like… for a fitting?"

Laughter poured from the other side of the phone, leaving me at a loss for words.

"Sure. A fitting. Among *other* things." With that, he cleared his throat, and suddenly, the serious, businessman version of Cliff was back. "Before I go, Cam. My proxy will be by in the morning with some pants I need tailored. Could he drop them off at the same time he picks up the tie? He has my measurements already."

I was still stuck on 'other' things and found myself agreeing without much thought.

"Sure. What time again?"

"Excellent. He'll be there at 8:30 AM your time. Thank you, Cam. I'll call you again soon. Have a good night."

And like that, the line went dead.

I remained in that state of euphoria for far longer than I should've, staring blankly at my plain white ceiling, cock flaccid and hanging out over the front of my pants. The fabric for my client's tie was sticky and crumpled beneath it, while the phone I had been clutching for dear life against my ear before was forgotten somewhere on the floor, leaving my hands free to dangle at my sides.

I thought he had been drunk, but at the very end of the call, he sounded sober and controlled, like we hadn't just had what was essentially phone sex between strangers.

I had phone sex.

I had phone sex with my *client*.

My first and *only* client for my new business.

Just imagining such a thing made me want to close up shop and move to another state. Knowing I had actually done such a thing made me want to incinerate into ash. Worse still, I didn't feel guilty about it. Not really. Like a teenager, I found myself thinking silly, lovesick things like:

Did he like it?

What if it was awkward for him?

Should I give him my personal number?

What if we get married?

I simultaneously wanted to kick my feet around in glee and kick my own ass. Unable to decide who I was in that moment, the only thing I could do was stare off into space, which I was doing with relish. The only thing that managed to pull me out of my embarrassing state was the clock on my phone. Checking the screen, I realized we were nearing midnight, and I *still* hadn't made the tie that was being picked up tomorrow.

It was then that I remembered what time he had said. 8:30 AM, 30 minutes before my recently determined hours of operation.

In a flurry of sweat, cum, panic, and embarrassment, I jumped out of my chair, stuffed my wet and uncomfy dick into my pants, wiped my hands with the soiled silk, and nearly tripped, making my way to the bathroom connected to the sales floor. As I fell into work mode and washed my hands, the pleasure and euphoria were steadily dissipating. Cliff wanted to meet me, and I would be lying if I said I didn't want to meet him.

But we barely had a professional relationship, let alone a personal one.

And my business was a fledgling at best.

How much was I willing to risk for a stranger? I couldn't say, and I tried my best to keep those hard questions at bay while I grabbed more fabric from my fabric wall and finally started cutting.

CHAPTER SIX

The following morning, I had much more clarity about what had happened the night before. And though it seemed Cliff wasn't bothered by it, I realized how bothered *I* was by it. I enjoyed the phone sex, and I was more than happy to do it with Cliff, but he was my client and a major one at that.

Was I going to allow myself to fall into personal relationships with every client?

This felt like a perilous path to start going down. While I hoped Cliff wouldn't go around telling everyone about what we had done together, I feared what would happen if he did. Plus, I wasn't interested in superficial physical relationships. Even if we did meet and have sex, there was a good chance he would move on to bigger and better things, leaving me far behind. I wasn't sure how I would handle working with him after that.

Maybe it was the fatigue from staying up all night to finish the tie, but I was much more cynical about it all.

As I mused over these what-ifs, far removed from the playful and romantic notions from the night before, the sound of my store door chimed. What followed was an older, unfamiliar voice.

"Hello? Is Cameron here?"

It was then that I recalled what Clifton had said just before hanging up:

My proxy will be by in the morning with some pants I need tailored.

I jumped out of my seat and plucked the box with Cliff's first tie nestled inside off my workbench.

My heart was thrumming so hard, it felt like it was coursing through my fingers, making them shake as I made my way out to the front. There, at the checkout counter, was an older man with salt-and-pepper hair. His face was sculpted with wrinkles, giving him a dignified and refined air. But his outfit was the exact opposite. His shirt was a garish yellow button-up with a bright red tropical flower pattern. His stiff and neutral expression was completely counter to such a playful shirt.

Similarly, his voice, as I gawked at him, was equally as cold and neutral.

"Good morning, sir."

I blinked, unsure what to make of this man before me.

"G-good morning."

The man frowned, holding out his hand.

"I presume that's Mr. Becker's tie?"

I nodded, robotically passing it into his proffered hand.

He squinted at the box, appearing displeased, even as he opened it and checked the contents. All of my confidence dissipated instantly. Was it that bad? I couldn't imagine someone wearing that shirt could hate that tie, but maybe Cliff wasn't as open to bold patterns as he had let on? I had encountered plenty of clients who said they liked one thing only to end up hating that very thing, but Cliff didn't seem like that kind of person.

My mouth was dry as a desert as I inquired:

"Is it bad?"

The man met my eyes, his gray eyes steely and cold.

"Not at all. Mr. Becker will love it."

I wasn't quite sure I heard him right. His tone was so aloof that I couldn't believe it. But once the meaning of those words finally settled over me, my heart soared. I had never felt such immense relief. I was ready to hide out in the back and take a nap when the older man placed a set of deep navy pants on the counter between us.

"These are the pants Mr. Becker would like tailored. The list of his measurements is in the front pocket. Can he expect them a week from today? I can also pick up any other ties made by that time."

I nodded, picking them up.

"That shouldn't be a problem."

The man nodded in return.

"Excellent. He will send payment by the end of the day."

And just like that, the man spun around on his heel and started marching toward the door, revealing his bright white shorts and yellow sandals. He looked like he was going on vacation instead of running an errand for work. It was pretty fun, but it was so counter to what I would expect him to wear.

Just as he opened the door to leave, he turned back to stare at me.

Quietly, he asked:

"Does this outfit... look strange?"

I shook my head.

"Not at all. It's really fun."

A light flush bloomed across his face, and I thought the corners of his lips turned up ever so slightly, but he turned back around before I could be sure. And just like that, he was gone.

I was stunned by the strange encounter, mainly because

of how cute it ended up being by the end of it. Just what kind of person was Mr. Becker working with a man like that? I had been imagining such a pristine and professional man, but maybe that wasn't the case?

This realization only made what we had done the night before all the more disturbing. I was lusting over and having phone sex with a man I knew nothing about. Well, nothing meaningful, anyway. He seemed very generous, positive, and friendly, and based on his taste and the people he hired, he liked quirky individuals.

My heart lurched.

I wanted so desperately to believe I knew him that as soon as I admitted to myself I didn't, I couldn't help listing out the minute things I did know — or that I presumed to know.

I swallowed as I lifted the pants off my counter, ready to look them over. I was fully intent on just checking to see what I was working with, but part of me was excited to have one more aspect of Clifton Becker that I would know — and this one was a physical element.

The fabric of the pants was thick and had a pleasant weight to it. They were high quality, no doubt. I was looking forward to seeing the brand, but as I let the pants unfurl and hang in front of me, I was distracted by something else.

The pants were wide. Just eyeballing them, the waist was between 40" and 42" with an inseam of maybe 36". He was over six feet tall, somewhere around 6'5", unless he liked saggy and long pants, which, judging by the brand and quality of the fabric, was unlikely. I had initially pictured him to be average-sized, probably muscular, and exceedingly masculine.

However, this pair of pants suggested he might be softer, pudgier, and towering.

He would probably feel really good in my hands.

I shook my head, trying to literally shake the growing lust from my fatigue-addled brain, but that image was still there — a tall, lumbering man with a soft middle.

As I turned the pants over, my eyes locked on the rear of the pants.

A soft lumbering man with an equally big ass.

Never in all my time tailoring and sewing had I been so turned on by a garment. But in all that time, I had also never had a client like Mr. Becker.

Trying my best to clear my head, I made my way back to my workroom. I set the pants down and pulled out the fabric I had planned to make his next tie with, deciding to take the opportunity to try to match it with his suit, but then it occurred to me.

His tie length was all wrong for a man his size.

Immediately, all lust evaporated away, replaced with horror at the thought of someone like Mr. Becker walking around in an impeccable suit, only to pair it with a skinny, measly strip of cloth. I was tempted to chase after his proxy and get the tie back so I could remake it to the correct length, but I doubted he would still be in the area. I couldn't pick up the phone fast enough, but as soon as I went to dial his number, I realized I didn't *know* his number.

Surely, I was mistaken.

I pulled out my notepad, flipping back to the front page where I had hastily scribbled down all of his requests the first time I ever started working in my studio, but only to confirm that I had never gotten his number. He had always called me first, never the other way around. I audibly cried out, slapping my hand over my face.

What business owner who takes commissions didn't have his client's phone number?

What guy didn't have his lover's phone number, for that matter?

But as soon as I thought about that last question, I realized Mr. Becker was not my lover or boyfriend in any sense of either word. My feelings had become far too entangled with my lust, and the reality of the situation had gotten away from me.

I didn't know who Mr. Becker was.

He didn't know who I was.

The fact that we had devolved into phone sex after only a few days of a transactional relationship was not a sign of a romantic one. No good could come from this, neither for me nor my business. Though my heart lurched, I knew what needed to be done.

I needed to draw a line in the sand, set up a boundary, and make it clear to Mr. Becker that I wasn't interested in a casual long-distance situationship.

Still, as I stared at the pants on the table next to the fabric I was going to use to make his next tie, I couldn't help feeling like I was about to lose something important.

~*~

Right on schedule, as day turned into night, while I was in the middle of pinning his pants to take them in around the thighs, my work phone began to ring. I had no doubt about who it was, and I was dreading hearing his voice. Part of me hoped he might be drinking again so we could avoid any serious talk for another day, but I was equally afraid I would end up falling back into sex and desire if he was.

I couldn't win, regardless. So, with a shaking hand, I picked up the phone.

"*Sew Cool Cam.*"

That deep baritone answered:

"Cam. Hi. How are you?"

Hearing him say my name sent a rush of shivers down

my spine. There was nothing better. But I had to refrain from falling into temptation. With a deep breath, steeling myself, I responded:

"I'm fine."

I tried to be distant and professional, even as memories of our last intimate phone call flashed across my mind's eye.

"My proxy just let me know he picked up the tie earlier. It's apparently really nice. I'm looking forward to it. But while I have you, I'm sorry about last night. I had a meeting with a client, and we got a bit drunk, but I think—"

I cleared my throat, loudly clipping off Mr. Becker's words so I could cut in.

"I've received your pants. I expect to have them done this evening. Is there anything else I can help you with?"

There was a heavy pause, enough to make me squirm. I wanted nothing more than to apologize and pretend I hadn't tried to draw a line, but finally, Mr. Becker responded:

"… is everything alright?"

My throat squeezed, my voice coming out much more nasally and shaky than I had intended.

"Everything's fine, Mr. Becker."

"Cliff."

My body reflexively winced. How many times had he asked me to call him that? How many times had I acquiesced? There was a part of me that would miss saying it, but another part was thankful I wouldn't have to. The less I said his name, the quicker I could hopefully move on from all of this.

We could be nothing more than strangers again.

"I think it'd be best if I called you Mr. Becker. You're my client, and this is a business relationship. I'd like to keep it professional."

There was a bullish huff on the other side of the phone.

"Wow. And here I was, hoping to ask you to meet up."

As I had expected, he wanted to meet up and, more than likely, have sex. That's all this was, a chance for him to get it in with someone of a lower station in life. I grew more and more comfortable with this decision as we went. The words that followed were much more even and controlled than they ever had been.

"I don't think that would be a good idea."

"Why?"

"A personal relationship between people with so much money between them seems a bit inappropriate... Doesn't it, Mr. Becker?"

"... Do you think I'm trying to buy you or something?"

It hadn't even occurred to me, but now that he had said it, it seemed reasonable. I nearly confirmed my newfound feelings on that, but Mr. Becker continued:

"I mean, I guess I can't blame you for feeling that way. It was a lot of money, but the money was for the work you're doing. Nothing else."

"How do I know that? Why would you want to meet someone you've never even seen before?"

He spluttered, filling the phone with static that made me wince.

"Never seen before?"

I couldn't speak. My throat and mouth were bone dry, and my heart was pounding so hard that it made my chest ache. I could feel it. Something was shifting, and I was about to be the bad guy in all of this. I just couldn't fathom why.

Finally, Mr. Becker chuckled — a cold and distant sound that lacked all humor.

"Your website. You have a whole 'About' page with a picture of you on it. That is you, right?"

My mouth was flooding with saliva. I was nauseous. I bobbed my head, unable to respond out loud even though he couldn't see me.

Thankfully, he didn't wait for me to respond, carrying right along since I couldn't have said a word even if I wanted to. But I could hear it in his voice as it wavered — he was having trouble speaking himself.

"After our first conversation, I looked up your store. I thought you were cute, then we started talking, and you sounded even cuter, so I wanted to meet. The call last night was a mistake, sure, but some part of me was hoping it would lead to something more since you reciprocated. I guess I was wrong."

I shook my head, my mouth gaping open, then closing like a fish. He wasn't wrong. Not at all. I wanted something more, and that was what scared me. Again, Mr. Becker didn't wait for my response.

"Did you look me up and see I wasn't your type? That's fine. You can say that — no need to imply that I'm trying to solicit you. I'm a grown man, Cam. I can handle it."

Somewhere, in the aching hollow of my chest, I was able to find my voice, though it was a whiny and pitiful echo of what it usually was. Tears were filling my vision, leaving it swimming, and I had to hold the phone to my face with both hands as they were beginning to shake.

Everything was falling apart, even though nothing had even been built yet.

"W-wait, Mr. Becker, I think I made a mistake—"

But he cut me off before I could continue.

"I get it. I'm sorry for putting you in that situation yesterday. You're right. We should keep it professional. I'll have my proxy come for the pants when they're ready. I'll try my best not to bother you unnecessarily, Cameron. Have a good day."

Before I could respond, the line went dead.

I couldn't believe how airheaded I was. It hadn't even occurred to me that he might have seen my picture. It was right there for anyone to see. My heart was jumping into my throat, and my mouth was swimming with saliva. I was going to puke.

With shaking hands, I pulled out my cell phone, opened my browser, and checked out my website. Right there, in the *About* section, was a trio of images. One was a more professional headshot of me, another was a candid shot while hanging out with friends on a hike, and the third was one I had taken of myself on the floor of my apartment, hand-sewing something. As if that wasn't enough, I had multiple paragraphs beneath, telling anyone curious about me who I was, why I started this business, and even personal details about what I enjoyed outside of my work.

Sure, I wouldn't say it was the exact equivalent of someone meeting me, but it was more than a stranger.

I could imagine a man who had to travel the world for work, reading about someone and becoming curious about them to the point of genuine attraction. It was probably a lonely life, moving from place to place, never getting close to anyone who wasn't an assistant or employee of some kind.

Yet, instead of trying to understand him when even I found myself drawn to him, I rejected him outright, even going so far as to suggest he was trying to *buy* me.

I lifted the landline phone, staring at the small, dim screen where his phone number had once been. Once again, I was reminded that I had no way to contact him myself to apologize, and I doubted I would hear from him directly any time soon — if I ever would again. He had any number of proxies he could probably use to keep an impregnable wall and uncrossable distance between us.

I swallowed, though it did nothing to stop the nausea still burning in the pit of my stomach.

Mr. Becker probably felt terrible, probably just as much, if not worse than I was feeling. But unlike Mr. Becker, who had someone else to blame for his pain, all I could do was blame myself.

CHAPTER SEVEN

I didn't hear from Mr. Becker again for a few weeks. His proxy came for his pants and a new tie I had finished within that time, and though he was as brightly dressed as he had been before, he was much colder. No matter how I tried to coax information about Cliff out of him, he coolly redirected me back to future tailoring requests. As I had wanted, Cliff was just a distant client.

I agonized, sometimes finding myself staring at the phone, waiting for it to ring and for it to be him on the other end, but I was met with silence more often than not. And when it did ring, and I answered it, I found someone else on the other end. Ultimately, I was consumed by anguish.

I didn't realize Mr. Becker had wanted to meet me.

I didn't know he might feel something between us like I had.

I just wanted to protect myself and my business, but all I had done was hurt someone who might have actually wanted to get to know me.

I had been alone for a long time, whether I wanted to admit it or not. I was so distracted by work that I hadn't

even realized just how much. But then I met Mr. Becker —
no, Cliff.

He had gradually started to change me. Even when I
was alone with my work, I slowly began to expect to hear
from him. What had once been a lonely and isolated
existence had been steadily invaded by this man.

But now, I was alone again.

And it was painful.

Each evening, I sat there, my heart pounding, my hopes
high, watching the clock on my phone, willing it to strike the
time when Mr. Becker would call. But the call I so
desperately craved never came. The landline remained silent
in its cradle. I was left alone in my dim studio, sad and
dejected, ashamed that I had let my fear of being hurt put
me in this situation.

So I spent my days in silence, working away on various
projects, including those for the very man I wanted to speak
to. The fabrics, beautiful and vibrant in the light, were dull
in my silent and dark workspace. Hot, heavy tears often fell
onto them, soaking in and leaving dark stains across
whichever piece I was working on.

Stained with loneliness and sorrow.

I could feel something inside me atrophying. Whatever
Cliff had warmed and made malleable was hardening into
something cold and painful. It made me nauseous, but there
was nothing to expel, so I was left reeling as I mindlessly
worked through the pile of projects on my worktable.

Just as I was drifting back into my growing loneliness,
the phone in the cradle rang.

I stared at the big brick of plastic. There was a twinge of
something in the cold rock within my chest — that flutter of
hope that had been steadily dying since the day Cliff had
hung up the phone for the last time. That sound, full of
static, followed by a deafening click, echoed painfully in the

recesses of my memory.

Part of me didn't want to answer, as I knew what would follow was more disappointment, but this was my business. As much as I wanted nothing more than to curl up and cry for a while, this had been my dream long before I ever came into contact with Clifton Becker.

I had lost him already. Losing this place by avoiding work so my feelings wouldn't get hurt would leave me irreparably destroyed. So, after what had to be the seventh ring, I took a deep breath, plucked up the phone, answered, and held it to my ear.

"*Sew Cool Cam*, this is Cameron speaking."

There was an intense, heavy silence.

Hesitantly, I repeated:

"*Sew Cool Cam*, this is Cameron speaking."

There was a rough and awkward throat clearing, one whose tone felt intensely familiar to me.

My heart jumped into my throat, but I held firm, unwilling to let myself believe it.

Then, he spoke:

"Hi, Cameron. I'm sorry for calling you so late. I just wanted to see if you could prepare a new tie. I would love it to match my—"

Before he could continue, I spluttered:

"Wait! Please. Let me say something."

Hot, heavy tears spilled from the corners of my eyes. The fabric I had been holding slipped from my fingers, and with my free hand, I uselessly swiped at my eyes. Nothing would stop the never-ending streams, and as hard as I tried, I couldn't stop the pitiful blubbering slipping from between my lips.

Cliff remained silent, though I thought I could hear the softest shushing sounds, like he was trying to comfort a frightened animal.

Whether it was real or imagined, I found a minute amount of comfort in it and was able to mumble my way through what panicked words I could come up with.

"I-I'm so sorry, Cliff. I m-made a mistake." I shook my head, though I was the only one who knew I was doing such a thing. "I was scared. I didn't want to mess up my business or get h-hurt."

Cliff cleared his throat, which I fully anticipated to be followed by unfeeling and neutral words.

How grateful I was to find I was wrong. Instead, I was met with warm and gentle tones, not unlike those I would expect from a parent comforting a hurt child.

"I know, Cam. I understand. I shouldn't have been so mean about it. It makes total sense why you would want to put a boundary between—"

My entire body jolted. I jumped up, slamming my hands on my workbench, sending various tools clattering along its surface and onto the floor. I even shocked myself with the sharp tone of my voice as I cried out:

"No!"

Everything was silent once more, leaving me to burn with embarrassment at my sudden outburst. Still, I swallowed, carefully managing my tone as I murmured:

"No. I don't want there to be a boundary between us." There was a shaky intake of breath on the other end, but no other sound. I continued, "I want you, Cliff. I know it's stupid— we haven't even met each other. But I want to meet you. I want to have the chance to make these stupid feelings... well... er... less stupid?"

All I could do was cover my face with my hand, willing the raging fire across my flesh to stop.

I was very thankful that Cliff couldn't see my pitiful reaction alongside the even more pitiful excuse of a confession I just made. To my surprise, though, there was no laughter or playful jeering. Far worse, there was intense silence.

My thoughts were racing. Why wasn't he saying anything? Cliff had always been jovial and enthusiastic, even leaning towards overbearing with just how charismatic he was. This was so unlike him that it made me sick.

I was trying to come up with anything to say to break the tension, only to be usurped by the man himself with a wavering voice:

"Why didn't you call me, then?"

He sounded frightened and sad. It was enough to make my heart lurch. With trembling legs, I sat back down, both relieved and guilty.

"I don't have your number. I wanted to call you as soon as you hung up, but I couldn't."

"You're on a landline, right?"

I nodded and murmured, incredulous:

"Yes?"

"Why didn't you hit redial?"

I blinked. I pulled the phone away from my face and glanced over the buttons. My grandmother had a home phone that I used to play with when I was young, so I knew the basics of how to use one, but I had never heard of the redial feature. Yet, as I looked at the bottom row of buttons, there, on the left, was a button that said 'Redial.'

If I could've melted into the floor, I would have.

With a sigh, I pressed the phone back to the side of my head.

"I didn't realize you could do that."

"… how old are you?"

"I'm twenty-four."

There was a sharp intake of breath and then a guttural clearing of his throat. The words that followed were stiff and cautious.

"I'm thirty-five."

Unsure of how to respond, I simply shrugged, only to realize once again that he couldn't see me. Embarrassed, I spluttered:

"That's nice."

There was a chilly silence for a few seconds after, only to be broken by a hearty laugh that instantly calmed my nerves.

"You should be more cautious of old men like me."

Something inside the pit of my stomach twisted. I thought back to our phone call — *the* phone call. The phone call that started this mess, and how I pictured myself dominating this man. I silently smirked to myself for a while, trying to withhold a laugh, until finally, I responded.

"I think you're the one who needs to be careful, Mr. Becker."

He noisily cleared his throat, coughing and choking as if surprised, then, as if he hadn't heard a thing, carried on with the conversation, though there was a slight tremor in his usual heavy, dulcet tone.

"Well, I guess if you haven't worked in an office environment, you might not know you can do that regardless of your age. I shouldn't have assumed. Here, I'll give you my number."

I fumbled through the fabric and papers at my workstation until I found a pen, which I used to hastily scribble down the number he gave me. Once I read it back to him and he assured me that it was correct, he said:

"Call me any time, for work or otherwise."

I swallowed.

"Can I text you?"

"Of course."

I smiled, all of the terror, embarrassment, and guilt finally melting away.

"Mr. Beck— Cliff?"

"Yes."

I breathed heavily before asking:

"Can we still meet up?"

His warm chuckle radiated around my head along with his response:

"I'd really like to, Cam."

I clutched the phone to my face, smiling so wide my cheeks ached.

"I'd like that, too."

"I'm glad. We can text about it. I'll also let you know what I called you about to begin with as soon as I remember what it was." He laughed, blanketing me in more of his overwhelming joy before continuing, "I've got to go, though. Have a good night, Cam."

"You, too, Cliff."

And with that, the call cut off. I pulled the phone away from my face and stared down at it, smiling as if it were Cliff himself. But more than anything, the feeling of that hard, cold thing that had steadily rooted itself in my chest melting away into something soft and warm was euphoric. Though I was once again in the silence of my studio, I no longer felt alone. On the contrary, I felt immensely fulfilled.

Though neither of us had said it, I felt loved.

CHAPTER EIGHT

Cliff

I just remembered what I was going to call you about. Can I get a tie for that suit you tailored?

ofc

is it weird for me to ask if you want to come see it when its ready instead of sending ur proxy???

Hahaha. Of course not. I'd really like that, actually. When do you think it'd be ready?

yayayayay

i can finish it in a cuple days then

Cliff

that work?

No problem. I'm buying my plane ticket now. Can you swing Wednesday?

yayayayay

np

this is really weird but can u send me a voice note??? im not gonna say y but pls????

🔊 ‖‖·‖‖·‖▶·‖·‖‖‖‖

thx🖤🖤🖤

You're such a cute pervert, Cam. Haha.

?????

no

wdym???

cliff?

its not anything weird ok???

cliff?

Hahahaha!

?????????????????????????????????

CHAPTER NINE

It was Wednesday.

We were open for business like any other day, but every time the chime at my door went off, I was jumping and skittering about, fully expecting it to be Cliff each time, only to be disappointed by another customer meandering inside. I was probably the only small business owner in the country to be disappointed by customers. But I was waiting for one specific customer.

My best customer.

Potentially, my favorite customer.

Clifton Becker.

Just thinking his name sent my heart pitter-pattering all around the inside of my chest. It was enough to make me dizzy, and I had to go sit down in the back for a while. There, on the table, along with his freshly tailored suit, was the tie that would go along with it. He was going to try it on in-store so I could make any adjustments, but part of me hoped that the fitting session might lead to something else.

I had suspected that Mr. Becker was out to take advantage of me in some way. Yet, here I was planning to take advantage of him instead. My face burned along with the organ pulsing in my pants, filling me with a confusing mix of embarrassment, guilt, and lust, all at the same time.

As I sat there, I fanned myself, trying to remain calm, or at least, in some semblance of that term, but that was turning out to be an effort in vain on my part.

Still, I tried, and as the chime went off at the front of my shop again, I held firm, simply calling out: "Welcome to *Sew Cool Cam*, be with you in a moment!"

I kept myself from jumping up and racing to the front like I had been, only to be met by a warm and familiar voice in response:

"Cam? It's me."

While my heart was racing, my body felt surprisingly sluggish. As the realization that Cliff was in person, in my store, settled over me, my muscles had grown taut. I shook as I stood, and each step awkwardly and stiffly 'clomped' against the floor as I made my way toward the front.

There, standing in the middle of the shopping floor, glancing around at the various racks of clothes and samples I had out was Cliff.

He was large, just as I had suspected after tailoring his pants and his suit jacket. And, just as I had *also* suspected, the ties I had been making were far too small for him, appearing as a thin, short strip of fabric disappearing into his buttoned jacket.

His jaw and cheeks were covered in stubble, and his hair was clumsily brushed to one side and generally unkempt. His face was similarly off-kilter, with a crooked grin, a slight pudge beneath his chin, and mismatched eyes — one brown and one blue. I had always assumed he would be this perfectly polished and refined man, but before me was a goofy, bright-eyed teddy bear.

He was perfect.

My heart thumped heavily in my chest as I stepped up to the counter, his gaze finally lighting on me. The corners of his eyes crinkled as his smile widened. It was pure, unadulterated joy, and it was squarely directed at me. I wanted nothing more than to leap across my counter, grab his face, and smash my lips against that grin, but the weight of my nerves rooted me in place, only barely so.

He whistled as he peered around the still semi-empty space.

"It looks so different than what I imagined."

I scuffed my foot against the low-pile carpet, nervous. My heart was thrumming wildly in the cavern of my chest.

"Is that a bad thing?"

He hummed, eliciting memories of our various phone conversations when he was just a nebulous being with a disembodied voice. Then, he shook his head and flashed a bright smile my way, a brilliant reminder that he was a real person. I could barely make out a single dimple on the left side of his face. It was charming.

"Not at all."

I swallowed, the following words sticking in my throat. I had practiced them, hoping to seduce and lure this man, whom I had grown attracted to by his voice alone. But now that I had the opportunity to use them, my mouth was drier than a desert.

Desperately swallowing, I croaked out:

"What about me?"

He was staring off at the far side of the room, starting to meander in that direction, away from me.

"What about you?"

Emboldened, now that his attention wasn't trained on me, I frowned, pouting a bit.

"Am I what you imagined?"

He froze, and his body stiffened. When he turned to face

me, I half expected disappointment or embarrassment, like he felt sorry that his answer wasn't what I wanted to hear. With that in mind, I winced, shutting my eyes to avoid seeing his reaction.

The silence was deafening.

I could hear the blood rushing through my veins, the soft, heavy thumps of my heart, and the adrenaline beginning to pour into my blood and fill my ears with a light ringing, all in painful clarity. At this point, I just wanted him to say anything, even if it hurt. Unable to take the waiting any longer, I opened my eyes into a tight squint.

There, Clifton stood in the half-empty space of my store, still smiling. His bangs had fallen out of place, resting in a short curtain across his forehead. He looked youthful, bright, and joyful. I wanted to bask in his aura. Then, he said:

"You're even better than I imagined."

This shy Cliff was not at all what I had imagined. On the phone, he was so loud and boisterous. Confidence radiated from him, and really, the moment I had seen him standing in my store, I could feel that same exuberance. But now, before me, as he avoided my gaze, he felt a bit like a stranger again.

Well, in many ways, he was a stranger either way, but *this* version of him — this blushing, seemingly virginal Cliff was more like prey than the man I had spoken to over the phone.

And I, no longer the nervous, clumsy, airheaded tailor, was the predator.

I closed the distance between us in three steps: one around my counter, the next across the floor, and the last to stand before him. As soon as he was within my arm's length, I reached for him, wrapping my arms across his vast shoulders and tucking my body against his soft form. Like we had done this a thousand times before, his arms went around my back, holding me flush, though I had no intention of parting from him anyway. His body was all heat, enveloping me entirely, alongside his citrus scent.

His shoulders hunched forward, ducking down so his face could meet mine, our noses brushing.

His breath caressed my lips, coaxing them open without a word.

Then, his tongue was in my mouth.

He tasted mildly of alcohol, like dark liquor, one of the few things I had guessed right about him. I imagined him on his flight, in first class, no doubt, with a heavy glass full of amber liquid. Before, he had been a faceless form that I made up on a whim. He fit perfectly in that form's place.

It was a satisfying flavor, though I wasn't a drinker. By the time our lips parted once again, my thoughts were fuzzy and thick like wet cotton balls. I imagined this was what it felt like to be drunk.

He panted, his gaze roving around my face, listless.

In a shaky, breathless voice, he said:

"We probably shouldn't do this out front."

I chuckled, shaking my head.

"You're right. Let's take this to the back."

Though he had suggested it, as I tried to pull away, his hands, resting on my hips, tightened. It was only with gradual pulling that I freed myself from his embrace, only to reconnect by taking his hand in mine. His fingers were thick and heavy. They were comforting.

I guided him toward my workshop door, hurriedly yanking him inside and shutting it behind us.

As soon as it was, our mouths clashed together again. His flavor filled me from the inside out, warming me right along with it. He tugged at my clothes with his meaty hands, yanking my shirt up so his fingers could explore the flesh along my waist. His hands were hot and pleasantly rough as they scraped along my skin, but they shook the farther they went up, like they were nervous or unsure how to proceed.

I wasn't doing much better. Every stitch of clothing on Cliff's body was tailored and fitted to his body, so the slightest movement pulled them taut and strained against my machinations. I feared that if I got just a bit too aggressive and excited, I would literally rip them off his body. That was a tempting image, but knowing how much he spent on my ties, I had no doubt that whatever he was wearing probably had an even higher price tag.

Just as I was awkwardly shifting my hands over the top of his clothes, trying to figure out where I could and couldn't touch him without damaging said clothes, his heavy voice erupted in a growl:

"Just rip it."

Guiding one of my hands between two buttons, he slid my fingers in that strained and parted space. I tightened my grip on the open section and yanked. Buttons went flying, clattering along the floor, but nothing was as satisfying as the slight whimper that whispered between those luscious lips and in that deep, tender voice.

"Yes."

That was all I needed. Nipping at his lips, I grabbed another section of his shirt and yanked. The fabric tore away with loud ripping sounds. There was his chest and his abdomen, a forest of hair. I dragged my fingers through it, admiring the supple flesh beneath until I reached the top of his pants.

There, I grabbed his belt and started yanking it off, all the while stepping toward him.

Each step sent him stumbling backward, and though he was much larger than I was, I strained to keep him upright, if only by his belt and the waist of his pants. Eventually, he found himself seated on the edge of my work table, where I could finally focus on undoing his pants. I yanked down his pants and underwear to reveal the throbbing morsel within.

As my eyes lit upon it, his entire body responded with a pleasant shudder.

It wasn't as small as I had pictured, but it was smaller than I would've expected from him. Everything he wore was dwarfed and strained by his size, and his penis was no exception. If I pressed my length against his, they would probably be about the same.

As I manipulated his member, his face contorted into the most pitiful winces, especially so when paired with his silent whines. It made me want to torment him. It was then that I recalled what was in my pocket.

I tugged it out, holding it up as if I needed to figure out what it was, all the while watching Cliff's reaction. His gaze was clouded, his mouth silently agape in ecstasy, but the moment he registered the tape measure in my hand, his eyes widened, and his lips shut into a hard line. It took everything in me not to laugh as, with one hand, I unwound it, letting the excess length fall across his abdomen.

"You came for a fitting, right? Might as well start here."

And with that, palming his cock, I lined up the tape measure against the shaft. The poor thing reflexively bounced, leaking thick, clear fluid from the tip.

"Six inches. Average. A bit disappointing."

He whined, his cheeks burning bright red even beneath his dark stubble. Crying out, he covered his face with his hands, arms quivering against his chest.

To my satisfaction, I was at least one inch larger than he was, which made this humiliation play all the more enjoyable. Clifton seemed to be enjoying it as well, precum steadily pooling into my palm, his dick showing no sign of going limp any time soon. It was then that I was blessed with a tantalizing idea.

Tutting with feigned disapproval, I grazed his head with the heel of my hand, making the man before me jerk and quiver.

"You're making quite the mess. We need to keep you clean for your fitting."

I took my tape measure and wrapped it beneath the head of his cock, pleased by the shocked gasps and slight shuddering of his thighs. It was pretty cute watching the engorged head puff up as I pulled the measuring tape tight beneath it.

Clifton, panting, parted his hands just enough so his mouth was exposed. What I initially thought was drool, I could now see were tears streaming down his arms and jaw, leaving little puddles pooling beneath him. While I took some satisfaction in seeing them, I stopped.

I had never done this before, and though I enjoyed all of the weak mewling and moans, I was suddenly concerned. In a much quieter and, hopefully, comforting tone, I asked:

"Does it hurt?"

It was only then that his hands finally fell away entirely from his face, revealing a cocky and taunting smirk beneath, though the area around his eyes was tinged red from crying.

"Not at all. Don't stop."

My flesh was suddenly alight with goosebumps. I wanted nothing more than to ruin this charismatic businessman.

"My pleasure, Mr. Becker."

And it was.

It was an immense pleasure.

Holding the end of the tape measure, I pulled upward, keeping his cock taut and at full attention. That smile of his faltered, only for an instant, so quick that if I hadn't been watching, I might have missed it. Then, it settled right back into that taunting, quirked brow and trembling-lipped smile.

This wasn't nearly enough for him, clearly.

And it certainly wasn't enough for me, either.

While I pulled his cock up, I stomped his pants down until they were ripped clean off, leaving his entire lower half bare. Reflexively, his legs spread, exposing his ass cheeks, bulging out as they pressed against the table.

I groaned, desperate to part them, shove my fingers in, and stretch him so I could fill him with my cock, but I didn't have a drop of lube. Glancing up into Cliff's face, his lower lip was sucked into his mouth, eyes watering and wincing as I occasionally tugged on the measuring tape tied around his penis. His gaze met mine, sparkling blue and brown, and swimming.

I yanked his cock upward, enjoying the snap of the tape as it went taut, especially when Cliff's high-pitched whine punctuated it.

It was a pained and uncomfortable sound, but as I watched his face contort with agony, the muscles in his chest and arms rippling, trying to refrain from reflexively reaching for his cock, I knew this man liked my torment.

If anything, he wanted more.

So, I took my free hand and sucked three of my fingers into my mouth, soaking them with saliva.

Only then, as they were dripping and shimmering wet, did I shove them between the cheeks of his ass, stabbing until I found his puckered hole. The tight muscle rejected me, doing its very best to squeeze and keep me from invading, but I pushed forward.

Cliff gasped, throwing his head and upper body back, tilting his bottom up so I could more easily access his ass, which I rammed over and over again with my stiff fingers. His body was squeezing around me, sucking at my digits, even as his hole did its very best to squeeze and snap them right off in return.

My spit was doing very little, but there was the softest of squelching sounds, taunting me. If I could just cum inside him, he would be perfectly wet.

As if he had read my mind, Cliff's legs widened, his voice pitched up into a bright keen as he cried out.

"Cam, I want your cock. P-please shove it in me."

My entire body was covered in goosebumps, and my cock was so hard it hurt as it pressed against the front of my pants. I loved audio porn. I loved having phone sex with Cliff, too, but nothing compared to the real thing, right in front of me, where I could see the tremble of his lips and the bobbing of his Adam's apple while he made all of those lusty sounds.

I wrapped the tape measure once around my knuckles to keep it taut while I pulled my fingers free from his now-gaping hole. With my free hand, I undid my pants and let them fall around my ankles while I tugged my dick free from my underwear. The beast that I uncovered was unrecognizable, even to me. I had been turned on before, but this was unbelievable. My dick was so red it was nearly purple, and pre-cum was steadily dribbling out of the tip like it was doing everything it could not to cum as soon as the air of my workroom hit it.

I hissed, jumping as electricity shot up from my shaft into my abdomen from even just holding it in my hand. I needed to get inside him as soon as possible. Otherwise, I was about to burst. Much more carefully than I had intended to be, I guided my bulging head to his hole, wincing as the muscle there flared and caressed my tip. Cliff wasn't helping things. His heavy, breathy voice gasping as our most intimate places touched.

With a shaking breath, I finally just shoved myself inside, shivering as my sensitive organ was suddenly enveloped in a choking warmth. My thighs quivered, the muscles in my abdomen rippling. I was on the cusp of cumming, and all I had done was put it in him.

Sweat dribbled into my left eye, burning it. I was somewhat thankful for the pain, as it was a much-needed distraction to keep from climaxing prematurely.

But then there was a shaking hand, wet with sweat, trying to wipe the sweat from my eye.

Cliff was panting, eyes half-lidded. He gave me a weak smile, like I had already fucked the life out of him, and he was beautiful. In his deep, gravelly voice, he said:

"I'm so happy we're finally together like this."

My chest squeezed. I grabbed his hand and pressed the palm against my lips, where I left a flutter of kisses. Then, nuzzling my cheek into his hand, I met his gaze and gave a smile of my own before I said:

"Me, too."

And with that, I began to move.

The sound of my sack slapping against his firm rear filled my usually silent workshop, a sound I had yet to encounter in any of my audio porn. It was a sound I didn't think I'd be able to cum without anymore, a raw, chaotic, and animalistic sound, when paired with the deep moaning of the man spread wide before me on my worktable.

It compelled me to ravage him — unrelenting and merciless.

I thrusted upward as if I might pierce through his soft abdomen. The tie I had so lovingly crafted for him had traveled up to hang off his neck and over his shoulder, shifting back and forth against the table as I fucked him. Where it was tied around his neck, the flaps of his collar had turned upward, and the thin fabric appeared uncomfortably tight. It was suddenly no longer enough to be inside him and strangling his cock.

I wanted to choke him elsewhere, too.

With a grunt, I flipped him over, his entire body trembling as I pushed his front down and into the table. The tape measure around his cock unfurled and landed on the floor, letting long strings of cum dribble out and pool between his feet. I could watch it for hours, but my cock was throbbing, aching for more.

Then, I grasped one side of his waist, pleased with how pliable and soft it was in my hand, while I reached for the tie, now splayed across the table. I took the familiar fabric into my hand, pulling it around so it would rest across his back if I let it go, but instead balled the end into my fist, taut.

"Are you okay with this?"

He was shaking, quivering, making his ass jiggle rather tantalizingly. But his head bobbed all the same.

"Yeah. I'll kick the table if I need you to stop."

So, I pulled. His breath rushed out with a final wheeze, and then there was a brief silence. What followed soon after was a nasally whine. Cliff's head turned, revealing his mouth, wide open, tongue lolling out as he desperately tried to take in air that wasn't going to come. His cheeks were flushed, hair sticking to his forehead and mussed against his neck. It was satisfying to see such a man fall apart under me.

Unable to hold back any longer, I started to thrust once more.

Immediately, those quiet, hushed gasps were much more desperate. Along with the squeaking of the table, the sounds of his choked cries filled the room. I shut my eyes, basking in it along with the shuddering massages his insides were giving as I thrust in and out of him.

The sounds he was making were almost more satisfying than the way he was squeezing my cock, though both had the pit of my stomach steadily turning. Pleasure was coiling there, burning, ready to burst. My thighs were burning, too, tightening, right along with my balls.

I was on the precipice of euphoria.

Then, just as his foot moved to hit the leg of the table, all of the tension that had been winding and winding in the pit of my stomach suddenly unfurled. Dropping the necktie, I pulled out, holding the base of my cock as cum shot out of the tip. It landed across his ass and along the entrance of his gaping hole, running like rivulets down his body until it dripped off and onto the floor with the rest of the evidence of our coupling.

Panting, I pressed my flaccid cock against him, letting my body melt. As my chest met his back, I could feel the tremors coursing through him, the rising and falling as he filled his lungs with the air that had been strangled out of him. He was much taller than I was, which I was just realizing was rather frustrating, as in my current position, I couldn't kiss his flushed and shimmering face.

Still, his eyes fluttered open, and he peered back at me, a weak smile blooming across his lips.

"Well… nice to meet you, Cam."

My face burned, and though I wanted to bury my face into his back, I refrained. He chuckled, reaching back to squeeze my arm.

"I'm serious, though. It's nice to see you and *finally* feel you."

I could hear it — the satisfaction and want lingering in his husky voice. It made my heart, heavy and slow after climax, suddenly erupt in uncontrollable fluttering. Unable to hide my embarrassment any longer, I finally buried my face in his back, taking in a deep breath.

The deep, musky scent of his skin was mixed with a sweet, citrusy scent, like vanilla and lemon.

Cliff's laughter reverberated through his back as he gave my arm one more gentle squeeze.

"I'm really happy, Cam. Very happy."

I let my eyes fall shut, soaking in those words. I was happy too. So very happy.

CHAPTER TEN

I was crouched on the floor, wiping up all of the evidence from our sexual escapades with a scrap of fabric I had leftover from one of Cliff's ties. Since meeting him, over the phone that is, I had used fabric for so many things it wasn't meant to be used for. Ashamed, I sopped up pools of cum, all the while silently praying for mercy from my tailor and seamster ancestors.

Meanwhile, lounging on one of my work chairs, Cliff watched.

I couldn't help glancing up at him, watching to see how he was, especially since we had gone much further and more aggressively than I had anticipated for our first time. But to my surprise, he seemed relatively unconcerned and unbothered. He was sitting up, leg resting over his thigh, a hand raking through his hair, while he manipulated his smartphone with the other hand. All he needed was a cigarette, and one would think he had just gotten done fucking someone rather than being the one who was choked, fucked, and ravaged.

When our eyes met, I reflexively looked away, my heart

fluttering up into my throat.

His eyes were striking.

The two different colors seemed like two different people were looking at me. One was serious and intimidating, the other piercing and cold — similar but different.

I wanted both of them.

As I crumpled up the soaked fabric and reached up to set it on the table that also needed cleaning, Cliff's heavy voice fell over me.

"I could support you, you know."

I blinked, glancing over at him.

"What do you mean?"

His foot was bobbing up and down like he was tapping along to a song only he could hear.

"I could invest in your business, help with advertising, and organize a workforce. I have 'fuck you' money, and I'd be happy to share it with you."

The idea of having a sudden influx of cash was enough to give me a brain orgasm. My mind was filled with cottony thoughts of rows and rows of fabric in varying patterns and colors. Maybe I could even have my own exclusive print made, create my own line with it, and sell it in my shop. I could hire people to pack things and sell my work around the world. I could even get a warehouse to store and ship from. The possibilities were endless.

But then I noticed Cliff still staring at me, an expectant look across his face.

As much as I didn't want to, I found myself suspicious of this man. What did I really know about him? Not much beyond our physical connection. We were moving much faster than we should have, and whether that was my fault or his didn't matter.

I needed to know what his intent was.

"What brought this up?"

He shrugged with a sigh.

"Seeing you on the floor, cleaning up jizz with silk scraps, is pretty depressing. It makes me feel like a shitty rich boyfriend. I'm an old man with a young lover. You should use me." He smirked, gripping the calf propped across his lap. "I want to make sure you know you can, since you don't seem to be the type to take charge outside of the bedroom."

He said it so plainly as if he had known me his entire life.

And the way 'boyfriend' fell so easily from his lips made me swoon. I had several boyfriends in the past, but never had I been so easily dubbed their 'boyfriend.' To have someone so willing to claim me as his, and presumably, let me claim him in turn, was such a romantic notion that it was hard to believe this wasn't just a romance novel.

It made my heart thump heavily against my sternum. Suddenly shy, I stared down at the floor, trying my best to maintain a deep frown that threatened to break into an uncontrollable smile. All while muttering:

"Who said you're my boyfriend?"

His calm and controlled visage faltered for only a second, exposing that small, simpering creature I had underneath me only a few minutes before. But like any decent and cunning businessman, he hid his face behind his hand, just long enough to stroke through his hair. By the time he was done, his face was back into that cold and unyielding mask.

I had to laugh, which seemed to calm Cliff, his shoulders falling ever so slightly.

Though he wore that cold and distant mask, an intensity radiated off him. I expected he might be about to scold me for my cruel joke, and I didn't think I'd be able to keep from crying if someone like Cliff got on to me. But then I caught a shimmer in the corner of one of his eyes. It appeared he was on the cusp of crying himself. So, I quickly jumped in, waving my hand and feigning a casual laugh.

"I'm just kidding." Once again, I began to muse on his generous offer. I wanted to grow my business, and the prospect of doing that quicker than I ever could on my own was a tempting one. But then I recalled my first official day on the job, when I was determined to work hard and put my own blood, sweat, and tears into building my business. I liked that person. I didn't want to lose them. So, with a sigh, I continued: "But while I appreciate the offer, I'm going to have to decline. You're my first and only consistent client right now. If you become my patron, I'll lose all my motivation to grow my business."

Cliff frowned, his body sagging forward, clearly disappointed. But then he said:

"That's too bad. Still, I expected nothing less from a new business owner like you. You don't need my money, but it's there if you ever do." Then, he winked, his single dimple appearing as he gave me a crooked smile. "Your tenacity and determination are a turn-on."

The hair on my neck stood up, my abdomen tightening as my penis suddenly began to swell. I had to actively, though as subtly as I could, press it down, trying to force it back into flaccid submission, though to little success. The only thing I could think to do was change the subject, and the first thing that came to mind was how this man had the funds to make all these generous offers, buy custom pieces, and wear suits from the top luxury brands.

So, in a slightly wavering voice, I asked:

"What do you do, by the way?"

"I'm the VP of sales for a talent acquisition company."

That conjured a nebulous image of old-time

door-to-door salesman, but I had no idea how talent acquisition played into that — or even what that meant. I couldn't imagine the man before me being successful going door to door. If I didn't know who he was and saw him towering over my doorstep, I probably wouldn't open the door.

"Cool... and that means?"

"I help my company get clients, then my company helps clients hire talent. Well, that's what I used to do. Now, I mostly travel the world, have really fancy dinners, go to far too many parties, and shake hands with client bigwigs, all while getting paid far too much to do it."

As much as I was attracted to him, the idea that the man before me, who had come in so haphazardly, was of such importance was hard to believe. I could definitely see him as a sales representative of some sort, but not much else. It was so unbelievable that I couldn't hold back as I muttered:

"There's no way."

Thankfully, Cliff took it in stride, his stoic face breaking out into an open-mouthed belly laugh.

"Yes, way. Look me up. I just met up with the CEO of a trucking company. They have me on their blog and everything."

With his permission, I no longer felt compelled to wait until he left to look him up. To my surprise, as soon as I put his name in, I was inundated with link after link, with his name leading every headline on a variety of company blogs and websites. Clicking into the first one, I was presented with a giant image of Cliff and an older man shaking hands over a conference table. He was beaming, his face freshly shaved, hair slicked back and shiny with product. His suit was impeccable, a deep purple with a pitch black shirt beneath.

The headline read:

Clifton Becker, VP of Sales at X LLC, Signs Ambitious Deal with X Trucking

Just when I was ogling him, in awe of his vibrant aura, I noticed the tie.

It was a wine-colored tie with a gold floral pattern, laughably thin as it disappeared beneath his buttoned suit jacket. Horrified, I realized it was the first tie I had made for him, and just as I feared, it was too small for him.

"Your tie!"

Unaware of my horror, he bobbed his head, smiling.

"Yeah, it was the first one you made for me. It looks great."

I shook my head, turned the phone, and showed him the picture. He didn't seem bothered at all, smiling at himself like he was looking at a nostalgic family photo. Frustrated, my next words were close to a growl.

"No. It's too small! Why did you request ties that size?"

He blinked, tilting his head to the side.

"What do you mean?"

I couldn't help shaking the phone in exasperation.

"There are different tie lengths that work better for people of varying heights. This tie length is for someone average-sized."

The left corner of his mouth twitched upward like he was about to bust out into laughter, which only further enraged me. But then he explained:

"But it makes my chest look *huge*."

I reflexively glanced down at his chest. He wasn't wrong. Now that his tie was back in its rightful place, nestled between his ample pecs, it certainly made them seem all the more appetizing. It also reminded me that I needed to see how much of the clothes we had torn up could be repaired. When I met his gaze once more, he had that cocky smirk plastered across his face.

"Told you so."

I stood up, tucking my phone back into my pocket. As I neared, he uncrossed his legs, planting both feet on the floor with his legs spread just wide enough for me to stand between them. He was so tall that even sitting, his mouth was perfectly in line with my collarbone. I took the tie in my hand, gently tugging it.

"You're not wrong, but I don't like the idea of other people seeing you like this."

His head tilted back, eyes half-lidded like he was in a trance.

"Is that so? Maybe you should make me some longer ones, then. But what will we do with these?"

I wrapped the tie around my fist, giving it a much sharper tug, which Cliff responded to with a groan.

"Do you have a side table next to your bed?"

He nodded, his Adam's apple bobbing as he swallowed.

"Good. Keep them there." With my free hand, I brushed my thumb over his lips. They were thick and velvety. "Now, open your mouth."

He did so without a complaint, and I shoved my thumb inside, clamping his tongue down into the bottom of his mouth. His eyelids fluttered before falling shut while a deep moan erupted from his open mouth. An electric current raced down my spine.

I was glad to be a business owner now.

I could close my shop and take care of my new pet, and no one could say a word.

With that in mind, I ducked forward, pressing my mouth to his, letting my tongue slip inside. Only then did I remove my thumb, and his mouth easily moved to match the rhythm of my own. I couldn't say how long we were like that, his rugged stubble scratching against my face as our lips parted and met over and over again, but it felt far too short a time.

I could kiss him forever.

While forever wasn't possible, I did close *Sew Cool Cam* that day to get as close to forever as I could.

~*~

Though I had declined my boyfriend's offer to financially support my business, that didn't stop him from helping me in other ways. Unfortunately, the day after our first in-person meeting, he was off on another business trip to another part of the country. He tried to explain to me the intricacies of the contract and the industry it was for, but most of the jargon went right over my head. All I knew for sure was that he was confident he could make the deal and that I needed to look out for another article online about it.

In the meantime, he called me every evening, just like he used to, but every day he started with an odd question:

"Received any new orders? Big ones?"

I had received new orders, but nothing I would classify as big. I had some elbow patch jobs, a local theater wanted some help tailoring old costumes for an upcoming performance, and I was working on new pieces to display in my shop windows. However, it was nothing that I hadn't had before, when I was exclusively online. That was until a week after he left.

I was, once again, looking up his name, and as he had predicted, his name was on a new blog. Much to my satisfaction, the main image was just Cliff. He was sitting in a chair, arms out in mid-movement, with his mouth open in mid-sentence. His blue eye shone in the light of the room, while his other eye seemed to be focused and honed in. He was open, playful, yet reliable and concentrated. It made the organ in my chest soar.

And, of course, I couldn't help looking over his outfit. As he had promised, he stopped wearing the too-thin and too-short ties, but to my surprise, he opted instead for a more open-chested look. The first few buttons of his light blue button-up were undone and pushed open to reveal the soft curves of his chest. There was an alluring amount of chest hair also peaking out from the top, really emphasizing how manly he was.

It was hot.

Too hot.

Equal amounts of regret and lust tumbled around in the pit of my stomach as I saved the picture to my phone for reference later. But then the bell above my store door jingled. I nearly tossed my phone onto the floor from the sound.

I wanted to slow my heart, which was jumping up into my throat, before I made my way out front, but then I heard a voice.

"Hello? Is Cameron here?"

It was a bright and cheery voice and entirely unfamiliar.

Coughing and wheezing with surprise, I rushed out front and behind the counter, only to find a young man standing there, peering around the showroom. It was a bit emptier than it had been, partially thanks to Cliff, who had picked out and paid for some things despite my refusal to take money from my boyfriend. Still, the young man continued to browse what was there, even after I cleared my throat to draw his attention.

Instead of looking my way, he reached out and started pulling off pieces from the racks. He'd pluck something down, stare at it with a furrowed brow and a deep frown, only to then put it right back. My heart was still racing, though not from surprise anymore.

I was getting pretty pissed off instead.

Once again, I cleared my throat, this time choking out a

rough:

"Hello?"

Thankfully, he responded this time.

"Hello. I was told to ask for Cameron. Are you Mr. Becker's tailor?"

Before I could calm myself and really take the time to understand what was being said, I stammered out:

"That's me."

Finally, he looked my way.

The young man nodded, stepping up to the counter and pulling out a binder from his backpack, which he pulled around and hung from his front. Papers and cloth samples spilled from the bulging thing, some fluttering to the counter as he shoved it into my arms. Panicked, I rushed to pick them up, failing to even question why he was doing this or who he was. More and more papers and things were still falling out of the binder, which weighed far more than any binder should. Thankfully, he read my mind, hastily answering my questions as he helped gather things and set them neatly in a pile.

"I'm Patrick Buckingham's intern. On Cliff Becker's recommendation, Mr. Buckingham would like an entire wardrobe for the upcoming Spring season."

The name Patrick Buckingham was familiar. But I was more focused on the other name. This must have been what Cliff had been referring to. My heart was soaring once more. Whatever this was, it was a gift from my lover, and that had me equally as excited as it did nervous.

Still, with a sharp intake of breath to cool my nerves, I set the binder down next to the stack of fallen papers and fabrics and then opened it up. There, front and center, was a picture of Patrick Buckingham, and instantly I realized who it was. He owned none other than the largest and my favorite porn site of all time, *PornyPeople.com*. He had started as a porn actor himself before moving on to start his own company, and though he was well-known for being naked, his social media had garnered plenty of attention for how stylish he was when clothed.

How Cliff knew Buckingham was beyond me, but as I flipped to the next page and found a contract proposal, which included a budget that far exceeded what Cliff had paid me, I nearly fainted. Bracing myself against the counter as all the blood drained from my face, I stammered out:

"Wow. Um. This is *a lot* to go through. W-when does Mr. Buckingham expect a response?"

The young man had pulled out his phone while I was busy losing my mind. He was typing something fervently into it while responding in a bored, blasé tone:

"The sooner the better, but he'll be expecting a response no later than Friday."

I swallowed, closing the binder with shaking hands.

"Sure. Friday. Sounds good."

The young man bobbed his head, never once looking away from his phone. Without a word, he spun around and marched right back out the door. I thought Mr. Becker had already turned my world upside down, but this was a whole other level.

As if on cue, my phone started to vibrate in my pocket.

Wiping my sweaty hands off on the front of my pants, I tugged it out to find Cliff's name plastered across the screen. I accepted the call and put the phone on speaker, unsure I'd have the strength to hold the phone to my ear.

"H-hey."

Cliff's heavy baritone rang out with perfect clarity:

"Hey. Get any big orders?"

I coughed, opening the binder in front of me again, just enough to bend down and peek inside. I couldn't see it, but I could feel it. There was a big order, for sure. It was the biggest I would probably ever have.

"I'd say so. How do you know Patrick Buckingham?"

His laughter echoed around my store, filling it with his warmth even though he was miles and miles away.

"Even the porn industry needs help hiring people, Cam. Accountants, developers, secretaries, sales reps — you name it."

I shook my head, even though he couldn't see it.

"You didn't have to do this, you know."

He sighed.

"I know, but I wanted to."

Part of me wanted to be upset. I wanted to work hard and achieve success on my own. Yet, at the same time, knowing I had someone willing to put their reputation on the line to help me like this made me incredibly thankful.

It was nice having someone believe wholeheartedly in me like this.

So, casting off any of my complaints and fears, I held the phone close to my mouth, whispering:

"I miss you, Cliff."

His voice was suddenly much deeper, grumbling out of my phone's speaker so deeply it crackled:

"I miss you more, Cam."

He was so far away from me physically, but with just a phone call, it was like he was right there beside me. His warmth, his positivity, and his love — it was all just a phone call away.

Thank you so much for reading!
I hope you enjoyed the story!

If you'd like to be notified when I put out another novel, please
check out my website:
books.evehealy.com